The Emerald Island

The moral right of the author has been asserted
A CIP catalogue record for this book is available
from the British Library.

ISBN 978-0-992-787-509

Printed and Bound by

Orbital Print, Sittingbourne, Kent

First published in Great Britain in 2013

by Princess-PM-Publishing

DEDICATION

For Shreya and Karan, who both inspired my
mind to wander back in time …

*Destiny holds a Rainbow Full of Dreams
Always Keep Believing …*

Chapters

Stories can only unfold...
when someone
fulfils an adventure

Chapter I

Mystical Mritsa Manor

'Welcome to Mritsa Manor, children, I'm Miss Deena, pick up your things and follow me,' came a voice from a young and very beautiful Asian woman.

As the children stepped out of a rather glamorous, long and shiny black limousine, Tristan Turner, Isaac Ellis, Mariella Jenkins and Evangelina Carter could never ever have imagined that what lay ahead of them would change their lives forever!

Standing on a large driveway designed in a reddish spiral, they could see that the grounds were full of bright, blooming flowers. They felt a cool breeze from the wind and then some gentle sprinkles of water fell upon them from a magnificent water fountain that was set right in the centre of the drive.

There they stood, right in front of the world famous Mritsa Manor!

Mritsa Manor was like no other. It was a very large and beautifully crafted building made of solid white bricks, complimented by sturdy white pillars covered adequately with surroundings of soft crisp, green ivy, giving a tasteful colour to this marvellous building.

There were four very wide front steps made of pure white marble, which led up towards a rectangular spacial porch to the entrance, to some very large arched white doors. It looked as if the manor was self-inviting visitors there - without having to make introductions.

In the centre of the triangular-shaped roof was an enormous black and white clock, happily ticking away. The numbers of this very important looking clock were set in bold black Roman numerals.

Set in an almost hidden location within acres of land, the manor seemed quite mystical, for this was a location that one could only possibly hope to reach by travelling for miles along a long grey, stony country lane.

Mritsa Manor was also very close to Lake Ullswater. The gentle sounds of the hissing orchard trees, when combined with the sounds of the soft, calm swishing noises of the lake, is what gave this magnificent manor such a peaceful aura.

It was autumn now and this was absolutely the best time in the world to see the unbelievable sights of the whole land, which blossomed in so many colours.

The surroundings of the manor were made up of many orchards containing various fruits and trees, all looking so alive, whilst revealing the beauty of their leaves. Swaying happily together in the cool and mild breeze, the spectacular view of colours were a mixture of bright auburn red, light orange, yellow, purple, brown and even some of the trees were still displaying a few leaves of fading green.

The grounds of Mritsa Manor were surrounded by a forestry of large green conifer trees, which were surrounding a hidden view of some tall reddish, brown walls. The entrances to the grounds were controlled by huge electric black coloured gates.

When the gates were closed, you could quite clearly see a large squiggly golden letter '*M*' which proudly introduced everyone into the manor's grounds.

'Wow! Just look around, this place is amazing, it's like stepping into heaven!' squealed Mariella, prompting all of the others to look at the beautiful site.

'Come along, children, there will be plenty of time to look around later,' laughed Miss Deena, as she led the children up the steps towards the front doors.

They walked past many hanging flower baskets which were made up of many colours and the smells of the plants were like a mixture of various perfumes.

'Please hang up your coats and take off your shoes, as we do not wear any shoes in the manor,' Miss Deena explained. 'This is to keep the floors of the manor intact,' she continued, as she led them towards a closet.

For indeed, anyone who entered this building could not miss seeing the exquisite black and white chequered marble floors that were so glossy and shiny, lighting up the entire large entrance.

This was self-explanatory as to why such a wonderful rule would ever exist!

Looking around in absolute amazement, the children first looked up at the high white ceiling which was decorated with interesting swirly black patterns, and then they looked at the large crystal chandeliers that were tastefully hanging, right above their heads.

They couldn't believe their eyes as they looked at the gallery of glossy walls which were mostly undisturbed, showing only a few superb mirrors, clocks and pictures. This entrance had a black and white colour scheme to it. Only a few plant pots could be seen neatly placed around the floor. They could see that the hallway would lead them to many other entrances, but those doors were all closed.

As they gazed straight ahead, they saw an enormous staircase with very wide steps. These steps were made of shiny black granite, which had speckles of gold sparkling from within them, which were supported by sturdy black metal banisters either side of them, clearly showing the way up towards the next level of the building.

'Wow, this is truly remarkable!' said Tristan, gazing around. 'The black and white colours remind me of a huge chess board. It's almost as though the whole room has the look of an adventure in itself and we haven't even seen anything yet!'

'Yes, it does look a bit like that doesn't it?' replied Miss Deena. 'The Professor is a very good chess player and because of his love for the game, he decided to design this entrance himself.'

Miss Deena was wearing a brightly coloured dress full of yellow primroses, which complimented her long flowing black hair, brown eyes, cherry coloured lips and olive skin.

The children stood to watch as they saw many men and women wandering around the manor.

Some of these people were visitors, whilst the others were the staff of the manor, all looking very active carrying out their various roles to ensure that the manor was always kept clean and maintained to its highest standard.

'Whoa! Do you live here, Miss Deena?' asked Isaac, in total amazement.

'Yes, I do, Isaac. The manor is a tourist attraction as you know, and I have been living here for some time now to help out the Professor. I really do enjoy staying here, but I will be leaving soon to return to my family.'

Miss Deena smiled, as she led them up the stairs. They all walked through a long hall, passing many rooms and noticing many detailed pictures on the walls as they passed. They also saw some very large brown Grand Father clocks standing upright on the floor, and there were also some smaller sized clocks quietly ticking away on the walls.

As they walked past the many rooms, they reached the very end of the corridor and stopped to look out of the large glass windows.

'Look at the gardens down there!' squealed an excited Eva. 'Look at all of those pretty flowers and look at those trees; they are shaped to look like animals, how clever is that!'

Staring out of the windows they could see so much more. Facing them were the gardens at the back of the manor, which were full of many exotic colourful plants and flowers. There were topiary trees of many animals. They could see the shape of an elephant, a unicorn, some lions, horses, foxes, rabbits, deer, and possibly even more, all spread throughout the greenery.

Scattered around the gardens were more superb water fountains, all flowing with bursts of water.

Further down at the bottom end of the garden, they could see what looked like a little tea room area, which was full of dainty white tables and chairs, neatly set out on a square shaped patio for visitors to sit and enjoy the view of the gardens.

The children could see that the bottom of the garden was also surrounded by tall green conifer trees, leading out towards the orchards. As they overlooked the gardens, they could also see a view of the famous Crystal Water Lake.

'Look how long the Lake is. I bet it flows for miles and miles and it looks so beautiful and very peaceful, doesn't it?' said Mariella.

'Yes indeed,' said Miss Deena as she moved away from the window. 'The lake is a very beautiful and mysterious place. Many years ago, the lake was given its nickname of Crystal Water Lake.'

'This is because so many people from all over the world who have travelled here, have stated that the water has felt very magical to them, and some have even said that the lake seems to have some kind of healing powers, and those who said they were experiencing troubles in their lives have stated that just by being near the lake seemed to make their life feel better. Some people, on the other hand, have said that they have sighted many things in the lake.'

Miss Deena led them forward. 'This area is our guest rooms; boys, this is your room and girls, you are in the room opposite. Put your belongings away and then I'll show you around and please put on your house shoes as the floors can be quite slippery.'

The children's guest rooms were of a large size, both rooms matching in decoration of black and white colours. They contained two single beds with two bedside cabinets either side of them, holding vases of fresh flowers. The rooms even had a sofa in them, which were set facing towards the large bay windows.

Various pictures were on the walls and there were large mirrored wardrobes in the rooms which made the rooms look even bigger.

As they put their bags into their rooms, they could feel the soft fluffy white carpets on the floor beneath them - which felt so soothing on their feet!

Putting on their house shoes, they followed Miss Deena back through the corridor, passing all the other guest rooms, and then back down the sparkly staircase to another part of the manor.

Miss Deena then took them around the manor, showing them all the different rooms, and Oh My! there were so many rooms! They saw many dining rooms, conference rooms, livings rooms, an extremely large kitchen, a large music room and a huge library too!

They reached a very big square-shaped hall, which had the tallest and widest windows that one could only ever imagine - if they were dreaming it!

The sunlight shone in so brightly, casting shadows onto the floor, and inside this room they could see more entrances to seven other rooms.

'This is the Professor's favourite room of the whole manor and he has named it 'The Hall of Treasures',' said Miss Deena. 'This room is where he spends most of his time when he is writing his novels. He also holds some of his lectures in here and behind all of those black doors that you can see are his spectacular showrooms.'

'They are filled with paintings, ornaments, gifts and many souvenirs that he has collected over the years, and some of the items are very unique objects that have been bought from many different countries. Wait here and feel free to have a look around, I am just going to let the Professor know that you are here.'

Miss Deena then left them in the hall and disappeared down the corridor.

The children walked into the centre of the hall which was sized similarly to a ballroom. The large room had white marble flooring and centered neatly on it was a rather exquisite red patterned square rug.

On the rug was an expensive glass coffee table which had sturdy golden legs, and surrounding this table were four black leather sofas with black and gold patterned cushions on them.

This room was always kept simple, immaculate and uncluttered.

Neatly placed in each of the corners of the room, were three tall Grand Father Clocks. There was also a large wooden writing desk, and an armchair facing towards the windows.

'I have never ever seen so many clocks in all my life, have you?' echoed Isaac's voice in the room.

'No, but I think I know why there are so many clocks in the manor,' replied Tristan, pointing up towards the red walls that were bordered in a gold colour.

They all looked up to see some very large black italic wording written across the painted red walls.

The inscriptions looked very important, meaningful and very glamorous. The children felt drawn to the walls, because they felt as though there was something quite magical about these words.

It was as though each of the meanings was a story waiting to be told, but as they stared again and again, they just could not work out what each riddle meant.

Reading out the three inscriptions from the first wall to the third, Tristan's voice echoed:

**'TIME IS OF THE ESSENCE
LIFE IS A RAINBOW FULL OF DREAMS
FORTUNE FAVOURS ONLY THE BRAVE'**

'Well, how fortunate are we winning an adventure of a lifetime and also getting to meet the Professor?' he added excitedly.

'Yeah, and we came here in a private limo too!' boasted Isaac.

The children were so excited that Tristan felt an urge to want to dance and then looked at Mariella and reached for her hands. Thinking exactly the same thing, Isaac followed by taking Eva's hands and together they all started to dance around the room, pretending to be professional ballroom dancers.

Turning and spinning around, they laughed and shouted together whilst listening to their voices echoing loudly. Their laughter and happiness filled the entire room. Staring towards the ceiling, they carried on dancing under the chandeliers and a large spinning mirror ball, which sparkled above them.

Round and round in circles they went until they finally stopped in front of the spectacular showrooms.

Feeling rather curious, they opened all of the doors one-by-one. Inside each room was a mixture of objects and gifts that the Professor had collected. The wonderful items were neatly arranged in the rooms and there were short descriptions of each thing written underneath them.

There were so many different things and the children started to look at a few of them, then began to read the little descriptions of the Professor's wonderful adventures.

Each room contained different and extraordinary objects of all kinds of things such as; musical instruments, paintings, sculptures, statues, ornaments, lanterns and so many souvenirs, just as Miss Deena said there would be.

'Look at all of these things! There's must be more than a hundred items in this room alone!' shouted Isaac, totally amazed.

Mariella looked at some of the paintings on the walls and she felt that each picture portrayed a story of a sad tale.

'Look at these pictures, they are so beautifully painted, but the people look so sad in them, don't they?' she said.

'Yes, they do, Mariella, I think these pictures are showing the history about the wars,' replied Eva, looking closely at each picture.

'Yeah, I think you're right, Eva, because there are some very old weapons in these cabinets and there are bits and pieces of war memorabilia all over the place,' added Isaac from the other side of the room.

Moving on to the next room, they could see a different theme going on in there.

'Wow!' shouted Tristan. 'This room is full of science objects. Look at that huge telescope and all of those pictures of the planets and the stars!'

'Yes, and look here, there's a chart of the zodiac and all of the meanings behind every star sign,' gasped Isaac, whilst also gazing up at the decoration of planets and stars that hung above him.

The next room was Mariella's favourite room, as it was full of china and porcelain dolls, puppets, clowns, fancy dress items and masquerade masks.

This was like a theatre room and it was full of dolls and puppets from all around the world!

'Oh, how lovely!' cried out Mariella. 'I wonder if these items are from theatres, shows and musicals that the Professor has been to see?'

'I would imagine that they are, Mariella. All of these things are just simply amazing!' replied Tristan.

The next room seemed to have such a peaceful theme to it. It was full of sculptures of men and woman from the Victorian times and beautifully crafted model angels, and there were also a mixture of various musical instruments.

The pictures on the walls were of landscapes, rivers and waterfalls and some of them were connected to plugs in the walls, which were switched on and the soft sounds of waterfalls flowing could be heard by all.

'Oh, I love this room. It just feels so peaceful in here!' shouted Eva.

The next room was full of dolls and other toys everywhere. There were old style steam engines, models of rockets, doll houses, racing cars and so many different toys that looked as though they had been collected from various places around the world.

The next two rooms seemed to combine their themes. They were full of items, some of which resembled happy things, whilst the other items resembled sadness. It was as if these two rooms were showing that in the Professor's life - not everything was pleasant.

Walking out of the seventh room they returned to the hall and sat down on the sofa.

'Oh, how brilliant is the Professor? Did you notice that the floors are made up of mosaic colours and each single colour of the seven rooms makes up the colours of a rainbow? Look! The first room starts as red, then yellow, pink, green, orange, purple and the last room ends in blue,' said Eva, looking at the others all nodding back at her in agreement.

'And look down on the floor, the sunlight is shining in and making the colours of the rooms form into the look of a rainbow! He really is a very clever man, isn't he?' continued Eva.

'Well I think this place is truly magical, it already feels like we are in a Rainbow Full of Dreams,' said Mariella.

Just as *those* particular words were uttered, a distant flash of bright light shone quickly through the windows, catching the attention of them all instantly.

They raced to the window to look for the intriguing distraction.

'Did you just see a light? I can't see it now, but it definitely wasn't the sunlight,' said Eva, puzzled.

'Yes, and I think it came from somewhere near the lake, but it's hard to see from here,' added Mariella.

'Maybe there's a lighthouse around,' Isaac remarked.

'Yeah, you could be right, Isaac!' replied Tristan. 'Anyway, we can have a good look around later.'

As they turned back around, they could see a tall, plump man with grey hair and spectacles entering the hall and making his way over to the window. He was very smartly dressed, wearing an expensive tailor-made black suit and, underneath it, a white shirt with ruffles covered by a dark waistcoat. A pocket watch that was attached to a golden chain could also be seen dangling from the inside of the waistcoat pocket.

The children returned to the sofa, watching this finely dressed man stand by the window with his back to them, fidgeting with his pocket watch.

He then turned around and bellowed out; 'Time waits for no-one!' and then he chuckled. Pausing for a moment, he then continued to finish off his sentence.

'Unless… it is asked to do so!' he said, making no sense at all.

'Welcome, children, please sit down. I am Professor Patrick Joseph Michael Dowley, but you can just call me Professor,' he said, chuckling again to himself.

The children looked puzzled upon hearing the Professor's very first words, and then they looked at each other a little bit oddly, and started to smile.

'I trust that you have all had a pleasant journey here and that you have got to know each other a little bit better? You must be Master Tristan, Master Isaac, Miss Mariella and Miss Eva. Am I correct?' he said, looking at them in turn.

The children nodded politely. Each child was aged 12, and they felt so lucky to be selected to come and visit the famous Mritsa Manor after entering a children's writing competition that had been organised by Professor Dowley.

It was almost coming to the end of their summer holidays, but the children couldn't wait for this day to come fast enough because they knew that they were going to be experiencing one of the best days of their lives!

Tristan, the youngest of four boys, had travelled with his parents and his brothers from his home town of Canterbury in Kent. They all travelled up to London to meet the other children, and to be greeted by Professor Dowley's designated and private limousine driver.

Tristan had slightly tanned skin with short wavy, black hair and brown eyes. He was a slender boy wearing a smart blue shirt, black trousers and black shoes. He looked very intelligent and seemed to be a polite and well mannered boy.

Tristan's father Marcus, was a doctor and his mother, Eleanor, a solicitor, so with both parents having excellent careers, Tristan was no stranger to seeing the finer qualities of life. However, his parents have always continued to teach their children to be modest, friendly and happy, but most importantly, to always remain respectful.

Being the youngest of the boys, Tristan was always used to copying his older brothers; Robert, Owen and Jayden, who loved playing football and computer games, reading superhero comic books and watching action films.

However, at quite a young age, Tristan became quite fascinated by watching his dad do magic tricks, when the family would spend many rainy days indoors. It was on his fifth birthday that he received a magic box set, a magician's cloak and a glow in the dark wand, which in time, made Tristan become quite the little wizard!

Tristan had spent hours and hours in his bedroom, practising magic over and over again, until he managed to perfect his little shows. He then started to learn how to juggle with beanbags and rubber balls, so that he could add a bit more excitement to his acts and make his performances look more fun.

So when Tristan found out that he had won a place in the Professor's competition, he was so excited because he was going to be part of a mystery adventure and he was also going to get to see the very famous Mritsa Manor.

Isaac was the middle child of three, sandwiched between two girls. He had an older sister and a younger sister. With fair skin and very blonde hair, Isaac also had the most amazing blue eyes. He came casually dressed in a white t-shirt and blue jeans and wearing black sports trainers.

He was quite small in height and had quite a curious nature. His vibrant personality made it very easy for him to make new friends because he always loved to chat. Overall, he was what you would call a happy and excitable boy.

Isaac had travelled down from Blackpool in Lancashire with his family. His father, Christopher, was an engineer and his mother, Cindy, a hairdresser.

He grew up in a terraced house which is so near to Blackpool's famous attractions.

Being the only boy, Isaac had absolutely nothing in common with his older sister Candice, who had just turned sixteen and her interests were only about music, boy bands, make-up, doing her hair and chasing after boys!

His younger sister Chloe was only eight years old, so she only loved to play with her dolls and dress up in fancy dress clothes and then play 'pretend princesses' with her friends.

So as you can imagine, Isaac had to find his own entertainment. He did love the usual boy stuff like football and computer games, but his favourite thing to do of all time was to go to Blackpool's Pleasure Beach with his dad at the weekends, because his father spent a lot of his time working there to fix any faulty rides or to fix various other mechanical machines.

Isaac loved living in Blackpool. He and a few of his friends were really quite lucky because they got to go on most of the rides for free, because his dad virtually knew everyone at the fairground.

So when Isaac got the call that he had won a place in the adventure, he was so ecstatic because he thought to himself, that no-one else could ever possibly love an adventure more than he did.

Mariella was born as a twin girl. She and her sister Maisie were both identical and both very slender girls. They had beautiful long, curly, dark brown tressled hair and they both had very stunning green coloured eyes.

Mariella came to the manor wearing a modest white summer dress, which was hidden under a pale blue cardigan and she was wearing white sandals. She had a sensitive type of nature that came with a beautiful smile, and her personality came across as a girl who always seemed to be happy.

Mariella and her family had travelled from Hertfordshire into London. Her father, Thomas, was a pilot, and her mother Annabel, a dance teacher.

Being a twin, Mariella spent so much of her time with her sister, as both of them had interests in virtually the same things. Mariella grew up as a very talented young lady from a very young age.

Being taught ballet and dance by her mother, she also had a passion for music and enjoyed taking piano, flute and guitar lessons.

Her home was a modest detached house; life inside it though, was always very musical and to Mariella, it always felt quite magical there, because it was such a warm, happy and pleasant place.

It was quite easy to see Mariella's sensitive nature shine through, especially when her mother would take her and her sister to Heathrow Airport to pick up their father. Mariella had a fascination for people in general.

She would happily sit for hours in the airport's V.I.P lounge and dreamily watch people from all over the world who had travelled in to London.

It would make her heart melt every time when she saw different people who were either friends or families running to meet each other before hugging, and then embracing tightly together.

Mariella and Maisie always had fun between themselves, by trying to guess which countries some of the travellers may have come from, and they both loved to see the mixtures of different clothing of the people who had travelled from all over the world.

When Mariella found out that she had been selected to be part of the adventure, she was very happy but also a little bit sad, as she was not used to going anywhere without Maisie, but she promised that she was going to have fun and that she would make sure she would share her adventure story with her sister as soon as she got home.

Evangelina was the older of two girls and she had a very special and close relationship with her younger sister Chantelle. Eva, as she preferred to be called, was a very pretty young girl with brown eyes. She had short reddish brown hair which bobbed around her shoulders.

She was slim and quite short, and she had a kind of tomboy look about her. Eva came wearing a long jumper draped over her jeans and she had white trainers on. She seemed to be a perceptive and very clever young lady.

Her father, Edward, was currently away, serving with the Armed Forces and her mother, Jennifer, used to own a cake decorating shop, but she sold the shop and started to work from home instead so that she could look after Chantelle who had fallen ill from a very young age.

Eva travelled down to London with her mum and Chantelle from Cheshire. Eva's home life was mainly living in rented accommodations, as she was used to moving from home to home so that the family could stay near to the army barracks where her father would be based.

Eva loved to go out and play with the local kids in the neighbourhood, but somehow, instead of doing the normal girly things, Eva preferred to climb trees and get dirty.

She loved to play games like hide and seek or cops and robbers, but whenever Eva played a game, she would always make sure that the rules were clear and fair for everyone, as she always seemed to have a good eye for seeing things clearly.

Eva also loved to spend time cooking and baking with her mum, but mainly she loved to play with Chantelle and would always make sure that her little sister was always comfortable and happy.

Eva had the kind of personality that showed that she liked to please everyone and she always put their needs first before her own.

When Eva found out that she was one of the winners of the writing competition, she was so pleased and so excited, because she had never won anything in her life and she so badly wanted to visit Mritsa Manor, because she had heard so many wonderful stories about it.

Adjusting his spectacles, the Professor's deep voice continued.

'Welcome to Mritsa Manor and congratulations to all four of you for being the winners of my competition. You are the ones who have been selected out of the many entries that I have received, regarding my competition. You four are the chosen ones who have been invited here to Mritsa Manor to experience the adventure of my new book - *'The Emerald Island'*.'

~ Chapter II ~

The Man of Many Riddles

*P*rofessor Dowley was no ordinary man, he was a pure genius! He was very famous for the success of writing many novels for many years.

The books that he had written, he had self-created from inspirations that were taken from a combination of his own life's adventures and from his pure imagination. His books were also very clever because his stories seemed so lifelike that they succeeded by allowing his readers to enjoy a feeling of disappearing into his marvellous adventures with him.

The Professor's well known novels were very exciting and somehow his storylines always seemed to nicely blend fantasy in with reality, which allowed him to successfully capture the attentions of a worldwide audience.

There seemed to be something magical about his books. People from all over the world had written to the Professor to tell him that after reading his books, they felt that they had become lost in the most wonderful fun-filled adventures.

Some readers even mentioned that they felt as though they too were actually there in his book - living the story themselves!

Because of such success and the unbelievable interest of the mystical Mritsa Manor, the Professor decided to make it a tourist attraction for everyone to see its beautiful sights.

He also cleverly decided to invent many mystery weekend adventures for his visitors to purchase and take part in solving his mysteries.

The manor was always a very busy place and now and again the Professor would hold competitions and invite the lucky winners to meet with him personally.

So these four children were so lucky. Out of the many applications that the Professor had received, they were the chosen ones!

'Before I give you the details of your adventure, I must explain to you the history of Mritsa Manor and how its beauty inspired me to want to create yet another wonderful adventure.'

The children sat and listened attentively as he continued to speak.

'As a boy I have had the fortunate pleasure to travel the world. My father was in the Royal Navy and together as a family, my mother and I travelled with him and have experienced the many cultures of the world. I have seen many good things in life but also many bad things too, but those experiences have given me a broad education and some great knowledge about life's little mysteries!'

Pausing, with his thoughts starting to wander back in time, he continued.

'When I became a young man, my father retired and we finally settled in England and my journey as a young boy urged me to study; Languages, Art, English Literature, Science and Astronomy. I then chose my path in life to become a teacher and I have travelled to many countries to teach children in places from all over the world.'

'Now children, when I moved here to the Lake District, my wife and I decided to pick the name 'Mritsa' for this manor. The name Mritsa has been chosen from the Hindu culture and it means 'Good Earth'. All that falls on good earth was the gods' intentions of keeping peace and kindness to all creatures, both great and small. As you have seen, the manor is decorated with topiary trees, exotic flowers, orchards and many marvellous water fountains,' explained the Professor.

'It has been designed that way so that all of my visitors can appreciate seeing the views of so many wonders of life living together in peace and harmony. It is important for you all to remember that beauty can surpass all evil.'

Just then, Miss Deena entered the room carrying a tray of refreshments and then gently placed the tray down onto the glass table.

'I have brought you some refreshments and some iced water,' she said softly. 'I find that water can be very refreshing and it can help to purify the soul.'

'Thank you, Miss Deena,' said the Professor.

'Please do join us as I would love for the children to hear you play your song.'

Miss Deena smiled in a shy but accepting manner and walked into one of the showrooms, and came out with a rather delicate brown wooden instrument looking similar to either a small guitar or a violin. But it was neither, it was a lute. This was a very old instrument, which dated back to the medieval years.

She sat down and began to play a song and the music sounded like a lullaby and it was very mesmerising to all who could hear it.

This song seemed to hold its own melody and meaning. It was a type of song that one could listen to and then realise that it did not need to have any words.

As the music played, the time on the clocks showed as 4.45pm. Suddenly all of the clocks in the manor began to chime at once as if they felt obliged to join in to compliment such a beautiful, sweet song!

Miss Deena, undisrupted by the sound of the chimes continued to play on until the song faded down to its closure. These additional chimes they could all hear had blended quite nicely into her song and seemed to add an extra exciting sound to the melody.

The children looked at one another very puzzled and when the music stopped, Isaac asked,

'Professor, do the clocks always chime early as it's not yet on the hour?'

'Good question, my boy!' bellowed the Professor.

'No, no they don't, they chime on each hour, as you will hear shortly. However, no-one knows what lies behind the power of music! Thank you, Miss Deena.'

She then rose from her seat to return her instrument to the showroom.

'I am going to arrange for your evening meals now, so I will come back to get you shortly,' she said, before quietly leaving the room.

'Okay, now I'm sure that you would all like to know why I have picked the four of you out of so many budding young writers?' asked the Professor, smiling at their puzzled but excited faces.

'Well, this year when I decided to write my new book, I needed to find some strong minded characters for my story. I have been looking for characters that have different personalities, dreams and ideas. So, when I set up this competition, the best of the best is what I have been looking for, but let it be known, that I have been very, very impressed with all of the entries that I have received this year, and it was an extremely difficult decision to choose who I have considered to be the best.'

'Professor, thank you so much for choosing us, we're all so excited to be here and your home is very beautiful, and this hall is amazing, this is your favourite room isn't it?' asked Mariella.

'Thank you, my child, and you are all very welcome here. Yes, my Hall of Treasures is my favourite room and I like to come in here when I want to sit and think about new ideas for my books. I have also held many glamorous banquets and masquerade balls in here and I get some very grand ideas in here when the hall has been decorated.'

'I also receive many letters from young couples, expressing their love for the manor and of its location. Many of them have written to me asking to hire out my hall for the reception of their fairytale-styled weddings,' replied the Professor.

He then watched Mariella's dreamy eyes wander around the room, as if she were taking it all in and happily dreaming, whilst picturing it all in her head.

The children sat there thinking just how really kind-hearted and truly marvellous the Professor was and now, they began to understand just how busy his life really was.

Apart from writing his books, the Professor also had to deal with so many different and wonderful events that were happening within the manor.

Just then, the clocks began to chime as normal on the fifth hour!

All four of the children remained silent. They did not question again how they had heard the earlier mysterious chimes, because to them just being there made everything seem so magical.

The Professor stood up and walked over to his writing desk. He opened a drawer and took out four objects, seven coloured circles and a scroll, and then he headed back to his seat in the centre of the room.

'If you remember back to the competition rules that were set out, it requested that all of the applicants had to write a short story about their own adventure and then explain why he or she would want to be in it. So, let me start with your story first, Master Tristan.'

The Professor then began to talk about each of their stories, one-by-one.

Tristan had written a short story, explaining that his character was a young boy who lived in a magical circus. The boy loved to do lots of magic tricks and was also very good at juggling. But one evening something very strange happened. A spell was cast over the circus by an evil magician. The evil magician's spell made everyone lose their magical powers so that he would be the only one to have them!

After this spell was cast, Tristan explained that he could not do any more magic tricks, but he knew that he had to save the circus. So, he cleverly tricked the evil magician by challenging him to play eleven circus games without any of them using any magic.

The rule of the game stated that whoever lost the challenge would lose their magical powers forever and would then have to leave the town. Tristan explained that through greed, the magician had forgotten that Tristan did not have his magical powers anymore and therefore agreed to play the games.

He explained that he and the magician played many different games but at the end of the tenth game, Tristan and the magician both had the same score.

There was, however, one last game to be played and that was juggling. The evil magician did not know how to juggle, but Tristan did!

So at the end of Tristan's story, he explained that he had won the challenge and the evil magician lost all of his magical powers and had to leave the town forever. Tristan said that he liked this adventure because it proved that his knowledge was far more powerful than magic.

'What a wonderful idea! Your story was very clever. I particularly enjoyed the ending where you have believed in yourself and how you have managed to win your adventure by using your knowledge and not by thinking that you have needed to possess any kind of magical powers to win. Therefore, because your story led you to race against time, I am going to name you as The Clock Master - The Keeper of Time!' said the Professor.

He then handed over a small pocket watch to the boy and said, 'Remember that it is always best to keep time on your side!'

Isaac's story was about an interesting adventure that he wanted to have at a funfair. He explained that he went to a funfair with his friends so that they could all go on lots of exciting rides.

Suddenly, he found out that each ride was very mysterious because when the ride stopped he found himself alone and that all of his friends had disappeared!

Isaac stated that when he got off from the ride he ended up being in a different fairground and even if he got back on the same ride, it did not take him back to the original fair! He then explained that he remembered that in every funfair there was a Hall of Mirrors.

If he could beat the maze of mirrors, then it would lead him back to his own fairground and back to his friends. Isaac said that he entered the maze and he had to depend on his memory to help him to get out of the maze. Isaac then explained that he loved to play memory games and said that he beat the maze, because he was so good at remembering things.

At the end of his story, he said that he liked this adventure because it had a lot of fun rides in it but also because he loved to play adventurous games.

'Marvellous invention!' boomed the Professor's voice. 'I really did enjoy reading your story, Isaac.

'It was fun and very creative and I absolutely loved your idea of disappearing on funfair rides and having to go into a maze made only out of mirrors. But what I loved the most was that you used your knowledge and your skill to help you to win your adventure. Therefore, because you are very skilful and not afraid to take on a challenge, I am going to name you as The Curious One!'

The Professor then passed him a kaleidoscope and the seven coloured circles.

'See what you must see, but only what you need to see, especially if you find that colours try to change your path!'

The Professor then moved onto the girls' stories.

Mariella's story was about her adventure in a place called Toy Land. She stated that she was a little ballerina doll living in a musical jewellery box.

One day, the music stopped playing in the whole of Toy Land and she was not able to dance and spin any longer, which made her very sad. All of the toys raced to see the Toy King to find out how to make the music play again.

The King said that the musical manuscript for Toy Land had been stolen by the Trolls who hated the laughter and happiness that music brought to Toy Land, because there was never any happiness in Troll Land.

The Toy King had said that the only way to bring back the music to Toy Land was to go to Trolls' Cave and save the manuscript.

Mariella said that all of the other toys were too scared to go to the Trolls' Cave, but the little ballerina doll wanted so badly to dance again that she decided to go alone and cross the bridge between the two lands to get to the Trolls' Cave and then save the manuscript.

When the little doll reached the cave, the Trolls came out and tried to capture her, but she was too clever! The ballerina doll started to dance and told the Trolls that their music was so lovely. The Trolls said that they could not hear any music, but the little doll insisted that they should dance with her so that they too could hear it.

So together, the Trolls and the little doll danced, when suddenly the dancing made all of the Trolls feel very happy. In fact, they liked dancing so much that they gave back the stolen manuscript to her.

The little doll then invited the Trolls back to Toy Land so that they too could enjoy singing, dancing and laughing. Mariella had explained that the people of the two lands became new friends and the music of Toy Land played once more, bringing happiness to everyone.

So, in the end the little doll was able to dance again. Mariella said that she enjoyed this adventure because she loved singing, dancing and playing music and also because she believed that happiness should be for everyone.

'Your story was sensational!' said the Professor, smiling at her. 'Reading your story has taken me back many years to when my daughters were little girls, as they used to love playing with their dolls, and they too used to dream up quite similar adventures stories like yours. My favourite part of your story was that you have remained very genuine about your love for music and dance and that you have a very good heart and a strong ability to see that there can be good in everyone. I am going to name you as The Melodic One!'

Then, passing her a silver flute, he added, 'Music can spell out a thousand words!'

Now, Eva's story was a very short story, but it was a very moving one. She decided to write about a dream that she had when she was six years old. It was an amazing dream that eventually did come true for her.

She had imagined herself walking through misty clouds to visit the Land of Dreams.

Once she had reached there, she walked through the Circle of Light to meet the Sand Man because he was the dream keeper and only he could make dreams come true. The Sand Man was everyone's favourite person because he had given so many people, so many wonderful dreams. But Eva explained that she did not go there to wish for any dreams for herself.

She said that she just handed over a dream to the Sand Man and then disappeared back through the misty clouds.

Eva then explained that she really enjoyed writing about her dream, because the dream that she had left with the Sand Man was a prayer asking him to make her little sister better. Eva said that after having that dream, a few months later and after having many treatments, her little sister became fully well again.

She stated at the end of her short story that she wished that the Land of Dreams was a real place, so that the Sand Man really could make everyone's dreams come true.

The whole room fell silent. They felt deeply touched by hearing Eva's story.

'I am truly lost for words, sweet young Evangelina!' said the Professor quietly. 'Your story is by far the best dream that anyone could ever have wished for. I was very touched by your words right the way through your adventure. I have also found it very touching that you were dreaming for your little sister at such a young age.'

'You have proved that fantasy does not always have to be a dream. In fact, your story proves that dreams can quite often become reality, and I am very honoured that you have chosen to share such a wonderful dream that has come true for you -

with me.' Then he added, 'I believe that you, Miss Eva, should be The Visionary One!'

He leaned forward and then handed over a small rounded shaped crystal decanter to her and then said, 'only when clear can it be used to protect you!'

The children graciously accepted their rather mysterious items and felt anxious to get started right away.

'So, now you all know why I have picked you,' said the Professor. 'You are all very imaginative, clever, and very strong willed, and I am sure that by working together as a team you will all do very well!'

The Professor stopped to take a sip from his glass and then continued to speak.

'Your quest will be to find the Green Monkey and return it to the Palace of Zeneka Island! Many years ago, a curse was put over the island by an evil man called Lord Zhakhan. He is the cousin of the king of the island and he has now captured and banished King Avinash. Lord Zhakhan wants to be the ultimate ruler of the world.'

'Zeneka Island, which is actually better known as The Emerald Island, was once full of peace and it was a place of beauty. It was full of wonder and full of life and it was a place where all humans and animals could roam around and be free from any danger. But, when Lord Zhakhan stole his reign over the island, he set a curse of darkness over the whole land. After destroying all of the island's beauty, he captured anyone who dared to enter his land. He has put a curse into the waters of the world and has created 'The Zielers', which are known as creatures of the sea.'

The Professor paused again for a moment and then continued to speak.

'Legend has it that after King Avinash's capture, his wife Queen Amia quickly escaped from Zeneka Island. After she disappeared without a trace, The Green Monkey - The God of Peace - also just vanished! Lord Zhakhan has been searching for many years to find the Green Monkey, so that he can destroy it. The Green Monkey is sacred and he is very powerful.'

'The Emerald Island became under threat when Lord Zhakhan used his grandfather's creation, 'The Goola Bala Swamp', to invade the island. He wants Zeneka Island to be his kingdom so that he can gain more power to eventually rule the whole world, but he cannot have any power unless The God of Peace has been destroyed,' said the Professor, describing his story.

'So, he has now sent The Zielers in to Goola Bala Swamp to seek out and capture Queen Amia, so that he can force her to tell him where the Green Monkey is. Zeneka Island is now surrounded by Goola Bala Swamp; a Swamp of Darkness that is empowered to fade the memory of anyone who poses to be a threat or a challenge against Lord Zhakhan.'

The Professor then stood up and handed over a golden coloured scroll to Tristan.

'When your quest begins be very careful! Lord Zhakhan is trying to destroy time all around the world. He believes that The Children of Time will be called upon to challenge him, so he will capture any child who dares to cross his path!'

'This is all I can tell you, but remember, with great knowledge comes great power and with time - memory will serve you well! Your quest will begin tomorrow morning at the ninth hour, but to win, you must find the Green Monkey before the final chime of the fifth hour. Good luck!'

Miss Deena came back to the hall and said, 'Come along now for your evening meal and then afterwards you can go and have a look around the manor.'

She smiled whilst looking at their faces all bursting with excitement.

After dinner, the children put on their shoes and dashed outside to look at the gardens and they were also very eager to head for the lake.

'Why do you think that the Professor always talks in riddles?' quizzed Isaac.

'That's because it's all a test, Isaac,' laughed Tristan.

'Well, when he handed us our own items, he then gave us each a cryptic message, didn't he, so I think that each of those sayings must have a meaning and I think that means we are going to have to use our items somewhere along the line, which should then eventually lead us towards the clues that we are going to need,' said Eva.

'Well, I think it all sounds really exciting, because the whole quest is in riddles, which is so clever, and he hasn't even given us any other clues, not even the first clue to tell us where to begin. So, he's making it more fun for us because that's just his way of making us think! I have never taken part in an adventure, so I'm really looking forward to it and I think it's going to be so much fun,' said Mariella.

'What do you suppose he meant when he mentioned Goola Bala Swamp?' asked Eva.

'I don't know, but it sounds awesome,' replied Isaac excitedly. 'I hope we get to jump into a pool of muddy gunge while we are looking for clues, and I also hope that the sea creature things that he mentioned, are going to be squishy sponge balls that we can play with and chuck around!'

'I'm guessing that tomorrow Mritsa Manor is going to be classed as Zeneka Palace and we will have to find the Green Monkey and take it back to the Hall of Treasures by 5pm. What do you think guys?' asked Tristan.

'Yes, you could be right there, Tristan, and I think that we may also have to try and find the king of the palace and free him along the way. It's so exciting because we will be searching for clues and we are probably going to be meeting so many of the staff who will be dressed up as all sorts of different characters,' replied Mariella, unable to keep the excitement from her voice.

'Read out the scroll, Tristan!' the others chanted together.

Tristan pulled at a red ribbon surrounding the delicate scroll and then by gently holding both golden ends, he started to slowly and carefully unravel it, revealing black italic writing from top to bottom. He then loudly read the words out:

**'TIME TAKES BUT ONLY TIME
MELODY PLAYS BUT ONLY IN CHIMES
NEVER SEEN AS IT SHOULD APPEAR
NEVER SEEN NOT ALWAYS CLEAR
EVER THE CURSE SHOULD IT BECOME UNDONE
ALLOWS THE COLOURS TO UNITE AS ONE'**

'That's all it says, but there are more words around the top and bottom of the scroll which say:

**'ONLY PURITY OF THE SOUL
MAY WALK IN VICTORY'**

The others gathered around and each of them kept reading out the riddle over and over again, feeling very puzzled whilst thinking of how they were even going to start the quest. Each child then looked at the objects that the Professor had handed to them.

'Well, we have a pocket watch, a kaleidoscope, a flute, a glass bottle and seven coloured circles,' said Tristan.

'And a scroll which makes no sense!' added Isaac.

'I think that first we have to look for clues around the manor and then as Eva said, we may need to use these items to gain more clues, then hopefully after we have found them all, the answers to the clues should then lead us to where the Green Monkey is,' said Mariella.

'Yes, I think that's right and I think he has put the riddles into a rhyme so that we can easily memorise it. So I guess that we are going to need to pay attention to everything that we come across guys,' replied Eva.

'Aah! But remember the Professor always talks in riddles, so we may not even be looking for a Green Monkey!' said Isaac cleverly. 'After all, surely that would be too easy to just go looking for things like a picture of a green monkey, or an ornament or even a statue of some kind?'

'Very true, Isaac,' replied Tristan. 'We will need to search for clues, but I think whatever we find will most likely lead us to another riddle and then another riddle after that, and maybe they will all just be never ending riddles because we can't find any of the answers! So I think we are going to have to part with our items just to gain better clues.'

'Yes, you're right, Tristan, because if we kept finding more and more riddles instead of clues, then we would just be going round and round in circles and we would probably lose the game and be caught by Lord Zhakhan!' replied Eva, laughing.

'Oh, but how clever is that!' said Mariella. 'I'm only guessing this guys, but as far as I know, in every adventure it's not always about winning, it's about how you play the game that counts!'

'So, who do you think is going to be Lord Zhakhan?' said Eva.

'I mean, we need to watch out for him so that he doesn't catch up with us, and also we are going to have to be very wise about our decisions as to which characters we are going to trust, along the way, aren't we? After all, we don't want to be led in to the wrong direction!'

'Good thinking, Eva, but I'm not too sure about that one yet, and plus, we're not going to find that out until tomorrow,' laughed Tristan, as they continued walking and admiring the beautiful gardens.

~ Chapter III ~

Mysterious Crystal Water Lake

$\mathcal{A}$s evening approached, the clocks began to chime on the seventh hour. Outside, the skies were turning grey and the winds were becoming quite gusty, swishing dust, sand and loose leaves into the air. The children walked around to the back of the manor to the magnificent gardens that led into the acres of land.

They walked down the main path towards a white arched fence which led them to another part of the garden.

Either side of the walk way ahead were large green topiary trees shaped as lions. They had been so cleverly designed to look as if they were seated and they looked so very bold and so very proud!

A sweet aroma filled the air, as this part of the garden was full of rose bushes, small plants and other exotic flowers of many kinds and in so many colours too.

They could see some smaller water fountains scattered around the garden as they followed a patio path leading down towards an exquisite pond full of tropical fish. There they saw some orange coloured koi fish, rainbow trout, goldfish, and so many other large and smaller fish swimming around. They also saw a few green frogs leaping from lily pad to lily pad.

'Welcome to the water garden,' said a voice from behind them.

The children turned around to see a tall, slim man heading towards them. He had brown hair and he was dressed in a white t-shirt which showed from beneath his blue denim dungarees. He happily whistled away as he walked towards them.

'Hello, I'm Joe, but call me J.J. My nickname is J.J. meaning Jungle Joe,' he laughed. 'That's because I spend so much time outside in the gardens.'

'Hello, J.J,' replied the children, each smiling whilst introducing themselves to him.

Jungle Joe was one of the gardeners of the manor and he loved his job so much. He looked like a very happy kind of person, always smiling, whistling and very chatty. He knew so much about gardens and he loved to tell his visitors all about the trees, the plants and the flowers. You could say that he really was a happy-go-lucky kind of man.

'How are you finding it all so far? There is so much to see and learn here, isn't there?' said Joe, smiling.

'Yes, there is and everything is so amazing, we all love it here,' replied Mariella.

'This place is certainly a lot bigger than I have ever imagined and the marble floors are so shiny that you could skate on them,' said Tristan.

'Yes, the floors are awesome, aren't they? Many of us have had a sneaky little skate in our socks at least once!' said J.J, winking and smiling cheekily.

'We really didn't know just how much goes on here,' said Isaac. 'How many people work here?'

'Oh, I would say at least one hundred people work here, if not more!' laughed J.J. 'There are so many events, tours, adventures, wedding receptions and so much more going on every day, that we need to have a lot of staff otherwise it would be impossible to keep the manor running. I am just one of the many gardeners that work here.'

'Those animal trees are excellent, did you make them look like that?' asked Eva.

'Yes, I did. I have been a gardener for many years and I have been styling topiary trees for about six years now. I am very lucky to be here because the Professor employed me after he saw some of my work at a garden show in London a few years ago.'

Jungle Joe was a truly talented young man. He started telling the children about the gardens and he knew all the names of every single type of flower, plant and tree. As the children looked around, he explained to them how much hard work was involved to maintain the gardens' beauty. He explained that each of the living plants had very different needs to help them to keep growing.

'The gardens are designed exactly in the way that the Professor described to us earlier,' said Tristan, amazed. 'He said that he wanted his visitors to enjoy seeing all of God's creations living happily together and this is exactly how it does look. It's brilliant!' he added.

'Yes, it is such a wonderful garden,' said J.J.

'This is where the Professor got his ideas from when he wrote his brilliant book 'The Gardens of Marvel'. It has an amazing adventure that began in this very garden and he has created the most wonderful characters in the story, just by taking ideas from here. It is my favourite book of his and if you haven't read it yet, then you really should do, because it is so exciting.'

'I have got his complete book set of - '*The Popple's Adventures*',' said Mariella. 'I love his stories about the furry animals and his books are so colourful.'

'I loved reading his story book - '*The Air of Mystery*'. It's the one about the little boy who comes across a deserted hot air balloon which takes him to so many different lands,' said Isaac.

'And I love his story - '*The Lost Princesses*',' added Eva.

'I've read all of those books too and now after seeing this garden, I definitely want to read - '*The Gardens of Marvel*',' said Tristan, looking at the others who were all nodding at him in agreement.

'I believe that your own adventure starts tomorrow, doesn't it, are you looking forward to it?' asked J.J.

'Yes, and we are very excited, because the Professor has set us on a quest to find a green monkey,' said Tristan, 'and he given us some objects that I think we will have to use along the way to help us to find the clues, then hopefully, we will be able to find the Green Monkey.'

'But we are not sure how to begin yet, because the Professor only told us a little bit about his new book and when he started talking, it was all in riddles and so far, none of it makes any sense at all!' added Isaac.

'Yes,' laughed J.J. 'The Professor is very well known to talk in riddles - but that's just his way of making the adventure more exciting for you. I am sure you'll have lots of fun working out the clues.'

'Well, we are all looking forward to it,' said Mariella.

'Are you going down to the lake? I'm just finishing now, let me put my things away and I'll come down there with you,' said J.J.

The location of the manor was so near to the lake and they could feel that the winds were getting colder, so they all went back to the manor to get their coats before meeting back up with J.J.

They followed him through the gates at the back of the manor, which led them into an orchard full of fruits; there were trees full of apples, pears, plums and cherries everywhere!

'Wow, there are so many trees!' shouted Isaac.

J.J. picked four apples from the nearest tree and passed them down to the children.

'There is a gift shop further down in the gardens and our visitors like to buy the home-made jam of these fruits. As you can see there are acres of land here and we also have quite a few rows of vegetables growing around here too.'

They carried on walking towards a steep gravelly hill, which was sloping downwards towards the shore of the lake. As they reached the sandy shore, they sat down to watch the lake glistening in the sunset.

Listening carefully, they could hear the soft swishing sounds of the water, calmly flowing back and forth underneath the approaching moonlight.

Taking a good look around, they stared up at the hill that they had just walked down and from a distance, they caught a glimpse of the black and white clock of the manor.

'Look! There's the clock of the manor, doesn't it look so far away from here?' said Tristan.

'Yes, it does, Tristan, but oh, doesn't everything just look so beautiful?' sighed Mariella. 'I could stay here forever and ever!'

'Yes, it's very beautiful here, isn't it? Tourists from all over the world love to come here,' replied J.J.

'Some of them are mountain climbers who like to back-pack up to the top of the mountains, and some people like to come here to canoe along the water. I have also seen many people come down here to bird watch, because the sky can be full of black ravens and some other wonderful birds, and if you are really lucky, sometimes it may be possible to see a few golden eagles flying around, but mainly a lot of people like to come here so that they can catch a glimpse of Mritsa Manor and also because this part of Crystal Water Lake has been known to be quite mystical at times!' said Joe excitedly.

'When the mists cover over the lake, many people who have had troubles or sorrows in their lives have visited here, and they have said that they believe that the lake is like a wishing well. They said that they found the lake to be such a calm and peaceful place to be, so some people have made a wish into this lake, and have then told the tales of their sorrows to the water, and some have even said that within a few months of telling the waters, all of their troubles slowly seemed to disappear,' added, Joe.

'Oh! What a lovely idea! What a wonderful, wonderful lake!' shouted, Eva. 'That sounds just like a dream that I had once,' she added, smiling.

'I am so glad that your dream came true,' whispered Mariella, giving Eva a big hug.

Looking at the lake, they could see that it was surrounded by very large Rocky Mountains. The mountains looked so high up that the children wondered that if they all climbed right up to the top, then surely it would lead them to a totally whole new world?

They stood on the shore to look around and then picked up a small twig that was on the sand. Each child then took it in turn to write their names in the sand. Horizontally, along the wet shore, they neatly wrote their names; TRISTAN, ISAAC, MARIELLA and EVA.

'The Professor loves coming down here. He said that the fresh air and the silence of the lake, gives him different ideas and inspirations for every time he wants to write a new novel. He also comes down here to have picnics with his family and he loves to play with his grandchildren,' said J.J.

'Does the Professor and his family all live here?' asked Isaac, curiously.

'No, the Professor and his family all live quite close by to each other in London. He has four children; two boys and two girls but they are grown up and married now, and they all have children of their own,' said J.J.

'Mind you, they do all come up here quite often to stay in Mritsa Manor. The manor is a family business, so it is mainly just used as a tourist attraction. The Professor, however, does come up here more regularly though, as he likes to write his books here and he is always invited as the guest of honour at the request of the couples who have been so lucky to have their wedding receptions here. I have seen some wonderful and very glamorous celebrations held here. They have mostly been English receptions, but in the past I have also seen a few Indian, Greek and Chinese receptions here too, and when The Hall of Treasures is all dressed up and decorated, it looks absolutely fabulous!'

'I bet that the queue to hire that hall must be as long as my arm!' shouted Isaac excitedly.

'I think the queue is probably even longer than this lake, Isaac,' added Tristan jokingly.

'When I grow up I am going to get married here!' squealed Mariella.

'So am I!' added Eva.

'The Professor and his wife Emily both chose to name the manor as Mritsa,' continued J.J. 'They met and fell in love in India when they were both working out there. They loved the Indian culture so much that they chose to name their manor Mritsa. India has the most superb and famous tales about the many gods that are worshipped there, so the manor is their way of keeping their dreams alive by being designed so extravagantly.'

'The Professor and Emily wanted a look for the manor which would symbolise the meaning of Good Earth. They then both decided to open it up to the public so that it could be a place for everyone to come and experience some of the most wonderful adventures that they have both had.'

'Oh, that's so romantic! I feel very lucky to be here,' said Mariella, looking at the others, who were also nodding.

'Well, this is Lake Ullswater and it is the second largest lake in the Lake District and it is about nine miles long,' said J.J. 'But, it was nicknamed as Crystal Water Lake many years ago, because so many people who have been here have mentioned that when the water glistens in the lake, the whole lake looks as if it has been lit up with lots of crystals.'

'Some people have even reported seeing some strange sightings here, whilst others have mentioned that some very strange things have happened to them here.'

'Strange things?' asked Tristan, intrigued.

'What kind of strange things?' added Isaac.

'When you say that strange things have happened here, do you mean that they are good or bad things?' asked Mariella.

'Oh, please do tell us J.J, it sounds very exciting,' said Eva.

'Well, it's very hard to know for sure if everything that you hear is true, but many people have said that they have seen distant sightings of sea monsters similar to the famous Lochness monster appearing in many parts of the lake, although everyone should really know by now that the famous Lochness stories were mainly founded in Scotland,' laughed J.J.

'Anyway, some have even said that when the lake is misty, they could see a shadow of a mysterious woman floating along the top of the water. You may have heard of her? She is known as The Lady of the Lake?' said J.J.

The children sat still, listening attentively. They had all heard about the stories of the Lochness monster before, but they had not heard about the mysterious Lady of The Lake!

'There have been many different stories about her, as some people have said that she is a vision of a young and very beautiful woman who is searching the waters for her family, whilst others have stated that she is the healing crystals of the lake who possesses mystical powers that help to heal the troubles of the many people who have been coming to the lake to find peace.'

'Oh! That sounds wonderful and sad all at the same time, J.J,' said Eva. 'Does anyone know if the Lady of the Lake has ever found her family?'

'No-one knows, Eva,' replied J.J. 'But, as I've said, there are so many different stories that surround the lake, I would imagine that only the people who have actually experienced anything really strange here, would be the only ones that could really tell us that. As far as I know, I've not heard anything myself, however, there have also been a few tales that I have read about, saying that some people have said that the lake has been known to make people disappear, but I don't think that's true,' he said laughing.

'Well, if any of the stories are really true, then I really hope that they all have happy endings,' replied Eva.

'There are many paintings of the lake inside the manor, have you seen them? They have been painted by so many people that have come here, and each painting reveals a different story that has been portrayed by the artist. If you look at each one very carefully, you will be able to see that the lake is painted quite uniquely by each person and the appearance of the lake changes all the time - it is as if the lake has been placed into a world of its own!' said J.J.

'Miss Deena has painted a few pictures too. She loves coming down here to paint and she also loves to sit on the shore to play her songs. The tunes have very sweet sounds and they echo quite beautifully across the water and many people have stopped here to listen to her play. I often make a joke with Miss Deena by calling her the Lady of the Lake!' he added jokingly.

'She played one of her songs to us earlier and it really did sound quite magical, but... the strangest thing happened when she was playing her song,' said Isaac. 'All of the clocks in the manor starting chiming earlier than they should have, and it sounded like... they were kind of joining in with her song!'

'Yes, I find that the clocks are quite mysterious at times. I too have heard them chime a few times earlier than they should, but I haven't really thought about asking the Professor why they do that,' replied J.J.

'Are there any lighthouses around here, J.J?' asked Tristan. 'When we were in The Hall of Treasures earlier we saw a light flash quickly through the window and it seemed like it was coming from somewhere near the lake.'

'Nope, there are no lighthouses around here, but many people have said that they have seen a light too, but no-one seems to know where it has been coming from. All I can think of is that it may just be the reflections of the water. If you do see any lights again, be careful not to look directly into them or you might disappear!' laughed J.J.

'Come on, it's getting quite late now, I'd better take you back to the manor before everyone starts thinking that we've all disappeared!' he joked.

When they got back to the manor, the children headed up to their rooms feeling quite tired, but they still felt so excited for the next day to come.

The following day, birds were happily chirping outside and the clocks of the manor started to chime on the eighth hour, waking the children.

They all hurriedly changed into their adventure clothes and then rushed downstairs for breakfast.

'Good morning, children, I hope that you have all slept well?' said Miss Deena, all dressed up in a lavender frock. 'The Professor has been called out to a meeting today, but he has asked me to tell you, that he will meet you all back in the hall at 5 o'clock after your quest ends. Stick together and I hope that you all have lots of fun and that you do manage to solve your quest. Good luck!'

After breakfast the children headed for the hall and sat down with their objects and the scroll.

They looked on the glass table and there was a note left by the Professor, which read:

'Remember, With Great Knowledge
Comes Great Power!'

Just then the clocks began to chime on the ninth hour!

'Well, this is it, guys - now the clocks, *really* are ticking!' shouted Tristan excitedly. 'Altogether, we have eleven items and I'll keep hold of this scroll,' he instructed.

'Let's look *inside* the manor first to see if we can find any clues,' said Mariella.

They raced around the manor looking in every room for clues. They recited the words of the scroll over and over again in their heads as they searched high and low.

They looked at the paintings and the pictures on the walls, they looked at every clock that they passed, and then they checked inside every single room of the manor to see if there were any other notes left by the professor that could possibly be the first clue. They hunted around for hours, but could not find a single clue!

So, they headed back to the Hall of Treasures and entered into the seven rooms. They examined absolutely everything from pictures to paintings, and then they looked at all of the ornaments and all of the other interesting souvenirs around.

They opened all of the pots and the boxes that they saw on the shelves and then continued to search through everything else. But it was still no use as they could not find any clues at all. After what seemed like hours of searching, the children sat back down in the hall.

'What on earth are we looking for?' grumbled Isaac. 'We've been hunting for ages now and there are definitely no clues in here!'

'Everyone put your items on the table and let's see what we can guess from all of the things put together,' said Tristan.

'*Never seen, not always clear*, that's what is written in the scroll,' said Eva.

Laying out their items, they recited the riddle of the scroll again and started to study each object, and then tried to make a few guesses one-by-one.

'Well, there are definitely no clues inside any of these rooms,' said Mariella. 'The only thing that is really clear is that all of the rooms have different coloured mosaic flooring and they make up the colours of a rainbow. The circles that we have are of exactly the same colours, so maybe we need to be finding something with a rainbow on it?'

Now that seemed the most sensible thing to do, and it was the best idea that they had, so they picked up their objects and all decided to look around the whole of the manor again to find anything colourful or anything that looked similar to a rainbow.

They all split up and Tristan headed back up the staircases, to check all of the clocks. He thought that maybe one of them could be in a different colour, or maybe even one of the clocks could be displaying a different time setting from the others - because it held a clue!

Isaac remained in The Hall of Treasures to check all seven rooms again. He thought that maybe something in one of the rooms may be missing one of the circles, so if he could find that item, then maybe the next clue would be there.

Mariella headed for the music room to check through the pile of musical manuscripts. She thought that if she could find a manuscript which had song words on it, then she could play her flute and try to recognise the song, which then might spell out, or maybe at least lead her towards, the next clue.

Eva looked at her glass decanter and remembered the part of the rhyme that was in the scroll that said, '*never seen, not always clear*'.

This made her think that she should be looking for other glass objects like flower vases, or any type of pictures that may have glass frames - or just anything that looked clear, because she thought, if things were not always clear, then surely she would need to be searching for something unusual because that item could be disguising the next clue!

So Eva wandered off into the kitchen first, and then headed in to all of the other visitor rooms to search for glass objects.

As genius as their ideas seemed - none of them could find any clues inside, so they eventually met back in the chess-styled entrance of the manor.

'Okay, well we've all looked inside, so now let's try *outside!* Maybe the first clue is hidden somewhere in the garden,' said Eva, sounding quite positive.

The children put on their coats and their shoes and headed outside to the back of the manor. The skies were unusually dull and grey on this murky autumn day and the high winds were strong in force, beating down on them.

'Come on, guys, we'll have to be quick before it starts raining down hard on us!' shouted Tristan.

'But where do we start first?' asked Mariella.

'Well, I suggest, that we should go to the furthest part of the garden first and then work our way backwards towards the front side of the manor. These circles that I have are all coloured, so let's look for anything like flowers, trees or stones that may have a colour on them and check to see if they have any clues on them. Okay?' replied Isaac.

'Yes, but remember to check and see if there are any words written on any of the walls or on the gates when you pass them, because we all know that the Professor likes to talk in riddles, so it may not be a colour that we are looking for, but another riddle, which may give us the next clue,' said Tristan.

'Great idea, Tristan, but I think that we should all split up, though, because there are quite a few gardens here. I'll go to the orchards first with Isaac, and you and Mariella look in those gardens over there, and then we can meet back by the water garden. Okay?' said Eva.

Through the gusty winds the children hurried about, continuing to search the gardens, when suddenly thunder and lightning lit up the entire sky, flashing over the gardens and over the lake.

'Look at those lights over there, Isaac!' shouted Eva from the orchard.

'Oh yeah,' said Isaac. 'Something is glowing over there and I reckon it's definitely coming from the lake! Tristan, Mariella, come quickly!' shouted Isaac.

The gardens began to look a bit scary in the stormy weather.

As lightning and the misty grey skies were casting their magic over everything, the gloomy dark weather was beginning to make the topiary animal trees look as if they were coming alive!

The children started to run through the misty gardens, passing topiary after topiary, flower after flower, and right through the bustling trees. They ran through the winds, through the chills and through the pouring rain until they finally reached the Crystal Water Lake.

Sure enough as they approached the lake, it lit up beautifully, light after light after light! As the lake continued to blaze like a bed of crystals, the water suddenly started to divide into two, allowing a path of water steps to arise from nowhere!

The view was totally outstanding. The beauty and the power of these watery steps caught the attention of all of the children.

Thunder and lightning became louder and louder and the rain continued to pour down hard. The winds picked up and became stronger and colder, but the children could not move. They stood still and became almost hypnotised by the lights that shone in the misty lake.

The lights were so bright and powerful that the children found themselves being slowly enticed towards the lake and into the watery staircase.

Walking in a trance, Mariella suddenly broke her gaze and then started shouting at the others.

'Don't look at the lights, get out of the water!'

But it was too late…..

Suddenly they could all feel their ankles being wrapped around and very tightly gripped by some strong black and green weeds. The grip of the weeds was getting tighter and tighter, pulling them downwards and sucking them all into the water.

The lake, now turning into stormy waters, started gushing and roaring along with the thunder and the lightning. The children tried to fight with the weeds, but it was no use. They were all sinking and could feel themselves being sucked downwards towards a porthole under the water.

For indeed, those lights that once appeared to look so beautiful on the surface, could now be seen under the water as the evil eyes of the sea creatures. They all had piercing eyes, and if you looked straight into them, they could quite easily blind your vision. They were strong black and green creatures, made of ropey weeds that tangled everywhere and they also had very sharp, snapping teeth!

The lake was no longer calm as the sea creatures made loud deafening screams that echoed loudly throughout the whole surroundings of the lake.

Spinning round and round and trying to catch air, the children were forced into a downward spiral as the water's pressure sucked them right in - deeper and deeper towards a windy tunnel. At an incredible speed the children whizzed round and round in circles, spinning faster and faster inside the tunnel.

All of them were sinking deeper and deeper and now, they were all sliding downwards, screaming and shouting for help whilst knocking from side-to-side, until they were finally zapped right into the centre of the lake.

Watching helplessly, they all looked up and managed to get one final last glance - for the once opened partition of the water that they had just seen, was now slowly closing back up and trapping them all inside!

Chapter IV

The Curse of Goola Bala Swamp

*T*he spinning of the whirlwind came to an end and the children were thrown out of the tunnel and found themselves landing with a thud right into a thick, gooey, muddy swamp - in complete darkness!

Emerging one-by-one, the children quickly helped each other out of the swamp.

'What just happened?' asked Isaac.

'I have no idea, I can't remember anything!' replied Tristan.

'Oh, it's so dark here, where are we?' said Mariella.

'I am pretty sure that it was raining before,' said Eva.

Shaking off the mud from their clothes, they stood up and started to untangle all of the weeds that still clung to them. The sky was very black and it was just too dark to see anything, but it was very quiet and the whole place seemed to look deserted.

'Look around you,' said Tristan. 'This place is completely empty, and there's no water around anywhere, and look over there, those trees are all withered. I think we must be on an island of some kind and I'm guessing there must have been a fire here because the ground is covered in ash!'

'Hello...o...o, is anybody here...ere...ere?' shouted Isaac loudly, as his voice echoed out in to the air.

'Sshh, Isaac,' said Tristan. 'We don't know where we are and we certainly don't want to attract any trouble!'

'Well, we can't just stay here, we need to find a way out!' snapped Isaac.

Eva put her hand in her pocket and pulled out a glass decanter which was somehow full of water.

'Look, everyone,' she said. 'I've just found this in my pocket and it's full of fresh water! I think I can remember someone once saying that water purifies the soul or something like that. Does anyone want a drink?'

The others then started to check their pockets to see if they could find anything and then one-by-one they all pulled out an item, but none of the children could remember what these items were for.

In fact, none of them could remember anything since coming out of the swamp!

'Look at all of these things we have, I wonder why we have them,' said Tristan, sounding very puzzled.

They passed the bottle to each other, but as it came back around to Eva, suddenly a single drop of water fell out of the glass bottle and splashed onto the edge of the swamp, causing it to react.

The swamp started to bubble violently, spitting out mud everywhere. Then it started to sizzle, hiss and fizz before bursting into flames. The children became quite shocked and quickly stepped away from the flames.

They stood and watched as it turned into a trail of fire which carried on blazing and continued to blaze down a track which seemed to go on and on for miles.

'Whoa! Look at that track of fire! It's going right round in a circle and it looks like it's going to surround the whole of the island!' yelled Isaac.

'Oh, no, now we're trapped here, whatever are we going to do now?' shouted Mariella tearfully.

'Don't worry, Mariella, we'll find a way out,' said Tristan, trying to comfort her. 'Come on, everyone, let's all go that way and see where that fire trail is going. It must be leading to somewhere, so if we follow it then maybe we can find a way out of here.'

The children put their items back into their pockets and started to walk along the sand in the direction of the fire trail.

'How do you suppose we even got here?' asked Mariella.

'I'm thinking exactly the same thing, Mariella, but I just can't remember anything other than us all being near a lake,' replied Tristan.

'It *was* definitely raining, and we were running to the lake for some reason, but then as we got there, everything just went blank!' recalled, Eva.

'Yeah,' said Isaac. 'Weren't we on an adventure of some kind, and I'm pretty sure we were meant to be looking for something, but for some reason I can't seem to remember what it is, nor can I remember why we even went to the lake.'

'It's all very strange, isn't it, but there's nothing we can do about it now,' replied Tristan. 'We are just going to have to look around and try to find a way out of here to get back to the lake.'

They continued walking in the dark, relying on the fire trail to be their guide, but the noises of the sizzling fire began to make them feel quite drowsy.

Suddenly, a voice boomed across the sky.

'Who dares to enter Zeneka? Who dares to enter my land? Babagashar, find the intruders and bring them to me immediately!' echoed a very loud and sinister deep voice.

'Zeneka! We're in a place called Zeneka! Run everyone!' shouted Tristan.

'Zeneka? Where on earth is Zeneka?' shouted Isaac as he ran behind the others.

'There's no time for any questions, Isaac, *run*! Just keep on running!' shouted Tristan.

Ahead they saw a dark forest and they ran towards it and found some bushes to hide in. Feeling quite scared, they all crouched down very low and kept very still and quiet.

It was dark in the forest but they could just about see around them because of the light that was coming from the distant fire track. They all took it in turns to peep through the bushes to see if anyone was coming.

'Where did that voice come from?' whispered Eva.

'I don't know, Eva, but it didn't sound very pleasant, did it?' Mariella whispered back.

'What do we do now?' whispered Isaac.

'I'm not sure,' replied Tristan. 'Let's just stay here for a bit. I think there may be some people looking for us, so we had better stay hidden in here until they've gone,' he said quietly.

Suddenly, they could hear loud galloping noises coming from a distance, which were getting louder and louder as they headed closer towards the forest.

The children peeped through the bushes and saw lots of men on horses approaching and, as they got nearer, sounds of deep voices could be heard ordering the grunting horses to a halt.

The children could see a burly, stocky, bald man, wearing dark clothes, standing close to the forest. He was looking at the fire trail and then he called out to the other men who started to gather around him.

'Search the grounds, men! There are intruders amongst us. Split up and find them immediately and then take them to Lord Zhakhan!' he ordered.

'Yes, Babagashar!' shouted the men.

The children did not dare to move. They watched cautiously as the men got back on to their horses. The men split up and then rode away in different directions, but the man who had been shouting before did not leave and was still very close by with a few of his other men.

'As you all know, men, today is the day! Today is the final day whereby the world will stand still and will be ruled by Lord Zhakhan forever and all of our powers will once again be restored!' said a man called Babagashar, as he gave out an evil laugh. 'We cannot allow anyone to stand in our way today so we must find these intruders immediately.' He shouted.

He then turned around and began to chant a few words to the blazing fire:

'Agun Baba, Jhollo! Jhollo! Kheo Dhukbena! Kheo Jhabena!' (Oh Father Of Fire, Come Alive! Come Alive! Let Nobody In! Let Nobody Out!)

He chanted very loudly in a different language and then he and the other men got back on to their horses and rode off.

The children waited for the men to disappear and then slowly came out of the forest.

'Did you just hear that?' said Isaac. 'I heard him say that someone called Lord Zhakhan wants to rule the world.'

'Yes, I heard that, Isaac, but who are they and what do they want with us?' replied Tristan.

'I heard him also say that today is the final day for something to happen. Oh, we must get out of here!' shrieked Mariella.

'I'm not sure that we can get out of here. I think that man was chanting in a foreign language and I'm pretty sure that he has told the fire to keep us trapped here, because look, the fire trail is now rising higher and higher!' said Eva.

'Well, we are going to have to find a way out of here,' replied Tristan. 'I just can't remember how we all got here in the first place, though, do you?'

The others all shook their heads as they could not remember how they had got there either and now, they also could not remember that they were meant to be on a quest.

For, unknown to the children, the reason why they could not remember anything is because they had fallen under the curse of the Goola Bala Swamp!

The children made their way through the dark forest, hoping to find a path that could lead them to safety.

They all knew that it would only be a matter of time before the men came back to search for them in the forest. They crept about slowly, trying not to make any sudden noises that would attract attention to them.

They walked very slowly until they reached the end of the forest. In the distance they could see some lanterns that were lit up in fire on the walls of a very large grey stone building that looked as if it was a fortress.

'Over here,' came a whisper from afar.

Suddenly, a young girl wearing a dark cloak emerged from nowhere and started running towards them.

'Quickly, come with me, Lord Zhakhan knows that you are here and he has sent his men to find you!' she said, almost out of breath.

The children were a little bit unsure of what to do, but they really didn't have any time to think about it, so they decided to run after her. As they followed her through a dark tunnel, they suddenly felt a shower of fresh water falling upon them.

This special kind of water from the tunnel was somehow cleansing them as they all ran through it, when suddenly, by some kind of miracle, their muddy clothes became washed and completely clean.

Racing through many other tunnels, they found themselves entering into an under-ground room lit only by firelight. As they followed the little girl into the room, all of the children suddenly felt very clean and dry.

Once inside, the little girl removed her cloak and revealed herself. 'I am Shrina,' she said softly.

Shrina was a small, pretty little Asian girl, with brown eyes, and long black hair flowing neatly down her back. She was wearing a dress made out of old cloths and she was bare-foot, but she had pretty yellow flowered anklets around both of her ankles.

'It is very dangerous for you to be here,' she said.

'How did you get here?'

'All we can remember is that we were all in a lake and then the next minute everything just went dark and we suddenly ended up in a swamp. I can't remember anything else,' replied Tristan. 'I am Tristan and these are my friends; Isaac, Mariella and Eva,' he added.

'Oh!' gasped Shrina. 'When you were in the lake, you must have been hypnotised by the Zielers!'

'Zielers? What are Zielers?' asked Isaac.

Just then a young boy came into the room. 'The Children of Time!' he said, approaching them all.

'Hello, I'm Kavi, I am Shrina's twin brother,' he smiled, greeting them all.

Kavi was a small boy with brown eyes and short black hair. He was dressed in a top and trousers that were also made of old cloths. He came in and placed a silver tray full of food and water down onto the floor.

'I have brought some food and drink in for you, sit down and then we will explain everything to you,' said Kavi.

The six children sat down in a circle on the stony floor and began to eat and drink, all of them now feeling so relieved that they were, for now - away from the clutches of Lord Zhakhan and his men.

'You have all been caught by the powers of The Zielers and they have brought you in to Zeneka Island,' said Shrina.

'Hundreds of years ago in India, the gods of the heavens were invaded by an evil curse. This curse was set by a man called Lord Vishru. He was once a very good and kind-hearted man and he was a very clever man, but in time and by using his great knowledge he became very greedy and wanted to have power over India.'

'He knew that some day, good would have to verse evil, so he made plans to try and create an unbreakable curse which would cause everyone to lose their memory and then become his slaves. He only had interest in gold, money and power,' she explained.

'So, Lord Vishru created a powerful potion to make memories fade. He then poured this potion into the waters of India, which then continued to flow into and affect the waters the rest of the world,' continued Kavi.

'Everyone became affected by his curse and India's beauty started to slowly fade away and it was not a peaceful place anymore. Lord Vishru then created a swamp called Goola Bala Swamp, which he named after his evil potion. This swamp has been circulating the poison of his potion beneath the waters for many years now and it has flowed into the waters of the whole world,' he explained.

'Oh, how awful and how wicked!' shrieked Mariella.

'The gods of the heavens knew that without peace, the whole world would be trapped by evil, so they united as one and, without Lord Vishru knowing, they created a secret island and named it 'The Emerald Island,' said Shrina.

'The royal families of India were sent to live here to be protected by the God of Peace, The Green Monkey, but Lord Vishru found out that the God of Peace was missing. He then also found out about the secret island and started to search for it, because he knew that unless the God of Peace was destroyed, he would not be able to have the ultimate power.'

'Zeneka Island is a hidden island and the God of Peace used his powers to make sure that the island's location moved places all the time, so that it could not be found. But regardless of this, for many years Lord Vishru continued to search but could not find the island. When he died, his sons and their sons for many generations have kept on with this search, all through greed of wanting to have power over the world.' said Kavi.

'Sadly, though, Goola Bala Swamp eventually did find The Emerald Island and now Lord Zhakhan has taken over. He has used the curse to surround Zeneka and this has stopped the island from being able to move. He then banished our father, King Avinash,' said Shrina, sadly.

'Oh, how sad for you both,' said Eva. 'Did he capture your mother too?'
'No, our mother, Queen Amia, escaped from the island,' replied Shrina.
'What about the Green Monkey, where did he go?' asked Tristan.
'The Green Monkey vanished, so that Lord Zhakhan could not destroy the powers of peace,' replied Shrina.
'Good for your mother and I'm so glad that he didn't find the Green Monkey either!' said Isaac, feeling rather pleased. 'So, how do we stop this Lord Zhakhan, because I'm ready to do battle with him?' he added boldly.
'Me too!' shouted the others.

'As you can see, our island has been destroyed and it is always dark here,' continued Shrina. 'Our uncle, Lord Zhakhan is the Lord of Darkness. He has burned down our beautiful palace and our beautiful land, and he then cursed the island. He has banished sunlight, so that nothing can grow here any more,' she said sadly.

'Although there is no daylight, time does still go on but can only turn in complete darkness. Now he has control of the island, he intends to destroy time all around the world by sunset today.'

'So that is what that man was talking about earlier,' said Tristan. 'He said today is the final day for something to happen and then he said they will all have powers again, but why today, what is so special about today?' asked Tristan.

'Because today is the hundredth day, the last day of another century!' said Kavi. 'Before Lord Vishru died, he ensured that every hundred years starting from the day that he began his evil plans, his curse of Goola Bala would be able to be used to fight for power - Today is that day!'

'So now Uncle Zhakhan is making sure that he does all that he can to stay in power. If he manages to destroy time by sunset today, the God of Peace will lose all of his powers whether or not Lord Zhakhan finds him or not, which means that he will have won and he will be able to put the whole world under his powers.'

'We also heard a man say a chant to the fire trail when we were in the forest, why did he do that?' asked Isaac.

'That must have been Uncle Babagashar, Lord Zhakhan's brother - he wants to have joint power with Uncle Zhakhan. He must have chanted to the fire to make sure that no-one else could get into Zeneka and that no-one could get out either,' explained Shrina.

'Wow! So are we in India?' asked Isaac, shocked.

'No,' replied Kavi. 'The island was caught under your lake about a year ago but it cannot continue to move unless Lord Zhakhan's curse has been broken.'

'So, have we been cursed by the Zielers too because we entered into the lake?' asked Tristan.

'Yes, you were caught by the curse of the swamp, but luckily, I found you just in time. The curse is not able to wipe out your memories completely, because when we ran through the tunnels you were all purified by the water, which will now help to slowly lift the curse from within you,' explained Shrina.

'Before our mother left, she protected the waters of the land. Zeneka Island was once full of many fountains and waterfalls which flowed beautifully all over the land,' she continued.

'The waters are very special and are very important to Zeneka to keep the land pure and away from any evil spirits. The water has come from our main fountain, which is named '*The*

Fountain of Innocence.' When mother escaped, the waters of Zeneka were protected and hidden in here and only Kavi and I can chant for their help,' she explained.

'So are you two both protected from the curse of the swamp?' asked Mariella.

'Yes, we are both protected and now Kavi and I have been separated from all of the other captured children, who are now known as *'The Forgotten Children'*,' said Shrina. 'Lord Zhakhan cannot wipe out our memories unless he destroys the Green Monkey, so therefore, he cannot break our mother's chants which have protected us from the curse of The Zielers.'

'The lights that we saw in the lake were so pretty and I can see why so many people would have been mesmerised by them,' said Mariella, slowly remembering seeing the lights.

'Yes, they would always look beautiful,' replied Shrina. 'The swamp lies beneath the waters, so when the Zielers are sent above the waters, they have the power to transform into anything that looks beautiful, *and* they have so many different deceptive appearances.'

'They can virtually change into anything like flowers or plants, or they can just transform into a lot of floating colourful petals... *and* as you all saw earlier - they too can glow up as lights! This is so that they always remain attractive to the eye,' said Shrina.

'Our father, Avinash, and our mother, Amia,' continued Kavi, 'are the king and queen of Zeneka Island. When the prophecy of peace was challenged by Lord Zhakhan, he sent out his sea creatures, which are called The Zielers, to surround the whole of Zeneka. The curse of the Zielers empowers the memory of the mind so that the people of Zeneka and anyone else that they have captured would forget all about Lord Zhakhan's crime. 'When he captured our father, he cast an evil spell over the whole island and then he banished our father into a whole underneath the ground.'

'Where father is at the moment, is where the Vortex is going to rise later on. Luckily, though, before mother left, she chanted a powerful prayer over the ground which is now protecting our father from any harm. Only when the hands of time are joined together again, can Lord Zhakhan's curse be broken and then our father can be freed.'

'So where is your mother now?' asked Eva.

'We don't know, but it's not safe for her to return here until the curse has been broken,' said Kavi sadly.

'Just how many children has he captured and trapped here?' asked Isaac, starting to feel rather cross.

'He has captured children from all over the world, there are hundreds of children here,' replied Kavi.

'But why has he captured them?' asked Eva.

'Because Lord Zhakhan is looking for The Children of Time,' said Kavi.

'The Children of Time?' asked Isaac, puzzled.

'Yes, the prophecy states that the Children of Time will be called upon on this very day to be his challengers. He knows that today is the last day that he can use his powers to win, so he captured all of these children thinking that they were the Children of Time and he has wiped out their memory! The prophecy states, that on the final chime of the fifth hour - only the Children of Time can challenge him.'

'He has captured so many children around the world, thinking that they are the children who could destroy his curse, but when he found out that they were not the Children of Time, he faded their memories and he has kept them all here as his slaves. He has trapped them all in the 'Chambers of Time', which is where they all are now. He has ordered them to make thousands of clocks, because he intends to destroy time at sunset today. At sunset, if he wins, he will set fire to the whole of Zeneka Island and when he has destroyed all of the clocks, then no-one will ever be able to challenge him again and he will be free to rule the whole world,' said Kavi.

'As you are the last children to be trapped here, you are our last hope of defeating Lord Zhakhan - You are all now The Children of Time!' said Shrina.

'Well, you can count on us,' said Tristan. 'We will help you to defeat him!'

'Yes, we will all help you,' vowed the others.

'Now isn't that strange?' said Eva. 'Our names spell out the word TIME! Tristan (T), Isaac (I), Mariella (M) and me, Eva (E).'

'Yes, you are absolutely right, Eva, and TIME waits for no-one!' quoted Tristan, as he slowly started to remember that saying from somewhere.

'We have these things in our pockets, I'm not sure what they are for, but maybe we can use them to help you?' he said.

The children pulled out the items that the Professor had given them and neatly spread them onto the floor, hoping that either Shrina or Kavi would know what to do with them.

There spread out on the floor was the pocket watch and the scroll, the kaleidoscope and the seven coloured circles, a silver flute and a glass decanter, which was somehow still full of water.

'Do you remember anything at all?' asked Kavi.

'No, sorry, all we can remember is that we were near Crystal Water Lake, but we really can't remember why,' replied Eva.

'We don't know why we have these things either, but I really do hope that we can use them to help you and I hope that we can also use them to help us to get back home too,' said Mariella.

'Yes we can use these, Shrina look! We can use these!' shouted Kavi very excitedly. 'Don't you all see? *You* have all brought the power to help us?'

'No, please do tell us what you mean, and you also mentioned a Vortex, what is a Vortex?' replied Eva, excitedly.

All of the children were now starting to feel very excited - thinking, hoping and praying that fate was going be on their side!

'The Vortex is where we will all have to go. It is the only place where good can verse evil. You are the Children of Time, not just because your names spell out the word TIME but also because your items are the essence of TIME!' shouted Kavi excitedly.

'Let me explain this to you. The pocket watch has been called upon to allow time to continue to turn, the kaleidoscope has been called upon to allow our eyes to still see the beauty from within us, the flute has been called upon to bring back peace and serenity to our land, and the glass decanter has been called upon to allow purity back into the soul. So together, although it may not seem very clear to you at the moment, your powers are the Essence of Time, and as today is the final day of the century, you have been called upon to help us to defeat Lord Zhakhan!' said Kavi.

'Oh, that's wonderful news!' said Mariella.

'I really hope that we can start remembering things very soon though, so that we can help you,' said Isaac.

'What about this scroll, can it help us?' asked Tristan.

'Yes, keep it safe, because we may need it later!' Kavi replied.

'And don't worry,' added Shrina. 'You will soon be able to remember things and then later on, hopefully, it will all make more sense to you.'

The four children felt very relieved and started feeling more positive than before. Although they still could not remember much of the adventure that they were supposed to be on, the one thing that they did all know, was that they had now met two new friends who desperately needed their help, so this was far more important!

Just then a loud patter of footsteps could be heard coming from the tunnels.

'Quick, hide your things!' ordered Kavi.

'The Gunda's are coming!' shouted Shrina. 'Stay together, everyone, and don't let on that you have been showered by the waters of the Fountain of Innocence. Okay?'

'Yes, okay, but who are the Gunda's?' quizzed Eva.

'They are Babagashar and all of Lord Zhakhan's men,' giggled Shrina as she looked at Kavi. 'Kavi and I nicknamed them as The Gunda's because they are bad men and we think that all bad people should be called Gunda's!' she said, as she started laughing again.

~ Chapter V ~

Zhakhan!
The Lord of Darkness!

'Quickly, tie these around your wrists, they will protect you from any further curses,' said Kavi, as he passed each of the children a black piece of coloured string.

All the children stood up quickly and tied on the strings and quickly moved the tray that Kavi had brought in so that the men could not tell that the children had been there for a long period of time.

The children could see shadows of burly men approaching the room.

'Aah! Now I can see why you both call them all Gunda's,' Isaac said with a quiet laugh, making everyone else laugh too.

'Well, whoever they are,' said Tristan, 'we will make sure that all of us together will save Zeneka Island and break Lord Zhakhan's curse forever,' he whispered.

'Shadows of the night, protect us from all evil forces of darkness,' whispered Shrina, as she prayed quietly.

'Seize all of them!' shouted Babagashar.

The stocky burly men captured the children and led them through the cold, dark tunnels through the fortress, until they all reached a large room which was in the centre of the fortress.

Thrown onto the floor, the children looked up to face a slim, tall Asian man. He was dressed in clothes made of fine black silk and he sat upon a red and golden coloured throne. Behind him they could see flames of fire, flaring up and sizzling.

The man had evil brown eyes, a thin black moustache and a short thin beard at the bottom of his chin.

'Well, well, well, what have we here?' bellowed an evil voice. 'I see that the gods of thunder and lightning have finally made our two worlds collide! Children of Time, you have dared to enter my land. Have you come here to dare to challenge me?' he bellowed angrily.

'Shrina and Kavi, you have both continued to defy me! You are nothing more than slaves to me and your powers are of no use and you will not be able to defeat me! Now you will both sacrifice the lives of yourselves, these children and the others and then you will watch me as I become the ultimate ruler of world!' His evil laughter made them all shiver.

'Your consequences will now banish and destroy your father forever,' he shouted. 'And as for your mother, Amia, she will be forced back here to serve me or she too will face her fate along with you father Avinash. Ha ha ha!' he laughed fiendishly.

Isaac started to look around the room. There were no lights on. The room was dark and he could only see through the fire light. There were many clocks hanging around the walls but he noticed that they were not ticking.

'Yes, boy!' shouted Lord Zhakhan, staring straight at Isaac. '*I* am Lord Zhakhan. *I* am the Lord of Darkness! Take a good look around because soon you will see that without time, darkness will rule daylight and my powers will be free to rule Zeneka, *and* I will also be free to rule the whole world forever.' Ha ha, ha ha ha..! The room echoed with his evil laughter.

Isaac began to hear familiar words in his head. It sounded like a voice was whispering to him, saying:

"*Remember, with great knowledge, comes great power!*"

Thinking very quickly, Isaac had an idea and then bravely spoke up.

'Lord Zhakhan, how do you intend to rule the whole world, sir?'

'What's this? I see that we have a curious one amongst us,' bellowed Lord Zhakhan.

Feeling in his pocket, Isaac took out the seven coloured circles and then spoke up boldly. 'Yes we *are* the Children of Time, sir, and yes, our leader has sent us here to challenge you. *These circles* that you can see here in my hands, have special powers and they will protect us against you. These circles are the colours of life and they have been brought here to protect the world. They are more powerful than you and you cannot break their circles of life. They have been bound by a colour code and if you can solve the code, only then will you be able to defeat us!'

'What code is this and who is this leader?' shouted Lord Zhakhan angrily. 'I know of no code of colours, but if this is true and if this is the challenge of the prophecy then we shall see what powers they will bring. I have no fear, boy, as you will soon find out when your code of colours will be defeated in the Vortex. Your spells will be broken and then whoever your leader is, I will destroy him!' He then turned to his brother.

'Babagashar, seize those circles, we cannot allow anything to stand in our way. I see that these children are going to be trouble, but I am the Lord of Darkness and those who have come here to challenge me will be the ones who will bow down before me and witness my reign of victory!'

Eva picked up on Isaac's very clever idea and she looked at Lord Zhakhan and by quickly thinking of how she too could make him feel uneasy, she spoke up to add to Isaac's story.

'Our leader is the Sand Man, sir! He is the ultimate ruler of the world! His powers are in *this very bottle*, sir. This is the Potion of Dreams!' she shouted.

Eva then reached into her pocket and pulled out the glass decanter which was still full of water.

Thinking very carefully and very quickly, she once again shouted, 'This is the Mist of Desire, and only the Sand Man can grant wishes if this potion can be turned into mist! This potion holds the dreams and the desires of the whole world and only the worthy will be able to know how to make that happen. Only then can the Sand Man be called upon to fulfil desires. We will be calling upon him to challenge you, sir!'

'The Potion of Dreams, you say? Hmm, well now, this Potion of Dreams is now mine and in my land, I am the only worthy one who shall bring forth this mist of desire. I commend your bravery, child, but your leader has no powers that can be greater than the Vortex, so this Sand Man will come to me and he will be powerless to challenge me and then you will all see how he *too* will bow down before me!' shouted Lord Zhakhan angrily.

Mariella could see that Lord Zhakhan was becoming very angry and then she too quickly joined in.

'Lord Zhakhan, it was those mesmerising lights which summoned us here sir, and it was also the sweet music of your land which has played its final song. The power of music is unbeatable sir - the power that lies within music, can spell out a thousand words! We have been called upon to restore the beauty that we can still see within the land. Your Zielers have already shown their beauty and that is how we have been called upon to come here. Your kingdom is very beautiful, and our leader has told us that beauty surpasses all evil.'

'I can hear sweet music playing all around your kingdom right now - and the music is spelling out so many words. They are so powerful, sir, that I can sense that they are spelling out the valuable words which are going to help *us* to defeat *you* in the Vortex! And, unless you are able to stop this music playing, sir, you will not be able to defeat us!' said Mariella smiling, as she kept looking all around the room, which made Lord Zhakhan become more and more angry and confused.

'What music? I do not hear any music playing. Babagashar, search the grounds! I want to know where music is playing and find out immediately what kind of beauty thinks it can challenge my darkness of fire!' he ordered.

Tristan, the last in line of all of the children, stood up to speak boldly.

'Lord Zhakhan, *I* am the Clock Master, *I* am the Keeper of all Time!' he shouted.

'Our leader has sent me here for a reason and that reason, sir, is to make sure that *all* of the clocks of the world will still keep turning! And that, sir, is exactly what they *will be* doing - continuing to chime, chime, chime! You have no power over me as this clock is far more powerful than you will ever know.' He pulled out the pocket watch from his coat and then started to wave it around in front of Lord Zhakhan.

'We have all come here to challenge you, sir, and if you are able to make time wait for you, only then can you conquer the world and try to make us lose our powers. We know that today is the last day of another century and it is the last day for the battle of power! So, I am here to tell you that at the final chime of the fifth hour - the final hour before sunset, *we will* defeat you!'

'I accept your challenge, you foolish and insolent boy!' shouted Lord Zhakhan. 'Master of Time, I will allow you to watch me as I destroy your leader, you and your friends and then the whole world! You are no match for me, boy, and you will find this out when you all face me in the Vortex. You will all be destroyed after the final chime at sunset!' He followed with a laugh.

'Babagashar, seize all of their things and throw them into the Time Chambers with the other children! You will all be my slaves and you can all have the pleasure of making the final clocks of time that you will watch me destroy at sunset today.'

Again he started to laugh. 'And as for you, Shrina, Caller of the Shadows, I will enjoy watching *you lose* all your powers of the night, and you Kavi, Master of Rhyme, will *no longer* possess your mother's spells of poetry!'

'You're wrong, Uncle Zhakhan!' shouted Kavi angrily. 'We may not know much about the prophecy or about the Vortex, but the one thing that we do all know is that today is the day where good will verse evil; we all know that you cannot single-handedly overpower the Vortex! You may have wiped out the memories of the forgotten children, but you have no power over me or Shrina!'

'Our father Avinash is the King of India and our mother Amia is the Queen and they are the rulers of Zeneka Island, *not you*, and now that the Children of Time have been called upon, together we will make sure that *we will* beat you at sunset and then the curse created by Lord Vishru will be defeated!'

'Kavi, Kavi, Kavi!' said Lord Zhakhan. 'You are just like your father in so many ways as you too are just as foolish as he is. He tried to challenge me in vain, but he could not defeat me and now he has been locked under the ground where the Vortex will rise, and as I will become the ultimate ruler at sunset, your father will be trapped there forever. My grandfather's curse has been growing stronger and stronger every year, Master Kavi, and *it will* continue to keep growing stronger every day.'

'This land is mine! It belongs to me and my family and I have been waiting very patiently for this day to come so that I can have what is rightfully mine and no-one, I repeat no-one, is going to stop me!'

'Uncle Zhakhan,' shouted Shrina, 'You have burned down our beautiful palace and you have destroyed the beauty of our island by replacing it with this ugly, monstrous looking fortress which bares only the signs of darkness and sorrow, but what you are forgetting is that beauty still shines from within our souls, so you cannot rule us!'

'All of these children that you have captured and hypnotised, are the sons and daughters of time and although you may think that your crimes are forgotten, you should know better than any of us, that *The Vortex* will not allow you to destroy anyone unless you are able to break its code,' shouted Shrina again, reminding Lord Zhakhan of her knowledge of the Vortex.

'I am the Power of the Night and Kavi is the Master of Rhyme, and now together with help from the Children of Time, we have gained even more power to challenge you. We may only be children, but as you well know, Kavi and I have both been blessed with our powers since birth, so, *you will never ever* be able to break our mother's blessings!'

'Sweet, young, Shrina! You are such a vision of your mother's beauty. However true that it may be that I cannot break your power or Kavi's, but the fact remains that I have stronger powers than both of you, so your insolence does not worry me. As you can see, I have indeed captured so many children who have been foolish enough to enter into the waters of the world, which have been ruled by my Zielers for so long and now these children are my slaves, as you all will soon be too! I believe that at sunset, I may not be able to wipe out your memories, but *I can* and *I will* banish you both so that you can join your father and be lost forever. The Children of Time will also become my slaves and my powers will force your mother to return.' Lord Zhakhan then shouted to his men,

'Remove those items and give them to me and take these children to the Time Chambers immediately and lock them all in and do not let them escape!'

The men quickly obeyed his wishes and then snatched away the seven coloured circles, the glass decanter and Tristan's pocket watch, and handed them over to Lord Zhakhan before leading the children away.

Lord Zhakhan left the room and disappeared into his laboratory to start examining these strange new objects. He began to feel very curious about how these objects could have so much power, and then wondered to himself how he could use them to make himself more powerful.

The laboratory was a very large and noisy room as different things could be heard going on at the same time; various machine-operated gadgets were clicking and spinning away at a fast pace, and there were sounds of coloured liquids, fizzing, bubbling and hissing away from many test tubes and from the big glass-shaped globes around the room.

His men were all around working the machinery to ensure that the solutions would be ready to be used in the swamp upon their victory.

For many years, Lord Zhakhan had been studying and perfecting his knowledge of science and chemistry, knowing that on the last day of the hundredth year, finally his time would come to use his brilliance to rule the world, as he had cleverly used the memory spell to make the human mind forget his crime.

He studied very hard and worked on creating various potions that would completely destroy time all around the world - for he knew that if he could do that, then the curse of the memory spell would not be able to be broken and then everyone would remain under his powers forever.

Looking at the coloured circles first, he studied them one-by-one. Sitting back in his chair, he sat with his hand over his mouth and chin, thinking back to the conversations that he had heard from the children regarding their powers.

He put the circles on to the table and thought about the circles of life that Isaac had mentioned, and just sat and pondered over the thought of a code of colours. He decided that he was going to follow the children's path in the Vortex.

He knew that if he did this, then he would be able to fool the children into breaking the code of the Vortex and then he would be able to overcome any power that the coloured circles may possess - and then, he would trap them all!

He next looked at the glass decanter. He was quite puzzled and wondered what powers the liquid inside the bottle had and how did it manage to escape past his Zielers in the swamp? He took a drop of the liquid from the bottle, and then under a microscope, he began to examine it.

Lord Zhakhan could see that it was just water, but then he remembered that his men had told him that the whole of the island had become a ring of fire when this liquid touched the ground outside.

He pondered very hard as to how this could work to his advantage, when all of a sudden a thought came into his head.

He knew then exactly how to do it! He would raise his own trail of fire in the Vortex once the children had broken the code and then they would not be able to follow him.

As he sat laughing to himself, he wondered who the Sand Man was and started to think how he could force this unknown leader before him and force him to serve under him. He decided that he would offer these new found gifts as a pledge to the Vortex to prove his worthiness to be allowed to enter, and then once he had entered into the Vortex, he would wait for this Sand Man to appear and make him do his bidding.

Yes… he thought to himself, as he was the one to bare the bottle, the Sand Man would have to honour *his* desires!

He decided that if he raised a ring of fire, then the Vortex could be tricked into allowing the liquid to touch the fire, which would then bring up the Mist of Desire, and this would also force the Sand Man to be called upon - then any desires that could be granted, would only be his.

Next he pondered over what he had heard Mariella say. How could she hear music playing in his kingdom and why could he not hear it? This power seemed to be a big problem for him, as he was not used to being faced with challenges that he could not see or hear to fight against. He remembered her saying that the lights and sweet music were mesmerising and that the words of this music could spell out a thousand words, but he did not quite understand how this could be possible.

Lord Zhakhan, thought about this one for a long time. As Mariella was the only one who had the power to hear the music, then she was going to be the biggest threat to him. He began to realise that the powerful music that only she could hear was possibly going to help all of the children to beat the Vortex and then defeat him.

So he decided that he was going to wait for Mariella to hear this music again and then when she had worked out the words that were required to decipher the code, he would then use her knowledge to beat them and conquer the Vortex.

He then thought about what she had meant by 'seeing the beauty in the land'. In his mind, he thought that this could not be possible, as he had covered the land with his spells of darkness!

Hmm, he thought, and then he decided that as it was the lights, music and the vision of beauty that led the Zielers to capture them in the first place and if it was colour that they were looking for, then he knew that the Vortex would be flashing in many colours.

That made him feel much better, because he knew that they would need their circles, but as he was now in possession of them, then amongst the flashing Vortex, it could be possible for him to trick them into going in to the wrong direction.

Next he picked up the pocket watch that was taken away from Tristan. He examined the watch very closely and remembered that Tristan had said, that this particular watch was far more powerful than he could imagine.

Lord Zhakhan knew that at sunset he was going to destroy time but then thought to himself that somehow, if this watch was so powerful, then he would not be able to destroy it.

He thought about Tristan saying, 'if you can make time wait, only then can you conquer us', but Lord Zhakhan knew that he could not think of any way to make that happen.

So, he started to devise a cunning plan to overcome this problem. Now he knew that Tristan, who had been appointed the Master of Time, would be the only person who would be capable of such a method and that was going to become a huge problem at sunset, so he would somehow need to challenge Tristan to make him lose his power over time.

He sat back in his chair and began to think about the prophecy of the gods. For many years, his ancestors had fought to have power but at the point of the last day of every hundredth year, the powers of God of Peace just could not be beaten.

The prophecy stated that if the God of Peace could not be destroyed - then by destroying time, was going to be the only way of gaining power.

As the Green Monkey had disappeared and as Lord Zhakhan could not find Queen Amia either, he had to make sure that nothing was going to be able to challenge him on the final hour before sunset.

The prophecy stated that the Children of Time would be summoned on the day for the battle of good versus evil and if the Vortex was not beaten - then no power could be gained by anyone.

Lord Zhakhan also knew that he would have to beat the Vortex, and he could only do that if he destroyed time and by looking at this powerful watch in his hands, he knew he needed to find a way to destroy it.

He sat back and thought that the watch was going to be too powerful to destroy, so he decided that he would also pledge the watch to the Vortex and wait to see if Tristan could still be able to stop time.

Yes! Lord Zhakhan thought - time can only be stopped when the code has been deciphered, so if the children solve the code, then he would trap them first, take the code and then enter it into the Vortex, then this would over come the powers of the watch and it would not be of any use anymore!

Rising from his seat he called over to one of his men.

'Go and fetch Babagashar immediately,' he ordered.

Five minutes later Babagashar entered quickly into the room.

'Time is running out fast,' said Lord Zhakhan. 'It appears that these Children of Time have come here with many powers, so there is a lot of work to do!'

'Yes, my brother,' replied Babagashar. 'We have put the six of them in the Time Chambers with the other children and they have been ordered to finish making the final clocks.'

'Good, but have you found out where any kind of music is playing?' said Lord Zhakhan.

'No, we have hunted in all of the rooms but we cannot hear anything, but we will keep looking,' said Babagashar before leaving the room.

Lord Zhakhan sat back in his chair pondering over the approaching battle at sunset. He pulled out a paper grid that was covered in black and white hexagon shapes, which looked very similar to the look of a chess board, but the only difference was that he had used hexagon shapes instead of squares. He had invented his own master copy of how he imagined that the path of the Vortex would be.

Now his knowledge about the Vortex was far more greater than that of any of the children, as he had paid great attention to the stories that he had heard about his ancestor's previous experiences of when they had to face the great and powerful Vortex.

Lord Zhakhan's knowledge led him to be aware that the challenge of the Vortex would not ever be the same as any other challenge that had previously taken place. He thought about how the children had turned up with their powerful items and then he realised that these items he had in his possession were the 'chosen ones' - they were the valuable keys that would be needed in order to work out the answers of how to get across the Vortex.

He then took out the seven circles and placed them onto the grid, and then he started to try and devise a route. Using the circles carefully, he moved them around the grid one-by-one as he began planning his own path to find a way into the centre of the Vortex.

As he looked at the seven colours, he then realised that he could not challenge the Vortex alone - the seven circles meant that there had to be seven players!

Although he devised his grid in black and white colours, he then also realised that the appearance of the Vortex would automatically change colours and, therefore, the path would change.

So he decided that he would make sure that when he entered into the Vortex, he would have to cast a spell onto his first stepping stone, to make sure that the colour of the stepping stone he was standing on would remain only as a black colour, but only until all of the children had entered into the Vortex.

He believed that the children were likely to know the right way, so he decided that he would follow their path and then, if for any reason they failed to break the colour code, he would then be able to quickly change his steps onto another path.

This would work to his advantage because if he pledged all of the children's items, then the Vortex may honour his path.

Next he thought about the gifts that had to be bared by all to the Vortex at the start of the challenge. He picked up the glass decanter but he could not think of how he would be able to use this item in the Vortex, so instead, if he presented it to the Vortex as a gift along with the others, then it would prove his worthiness to enter into the challenge.

Yes, he thought, this way the Vortex would bring up the Mist of Desire that Eva had mentioned and then if there was such a leader called the Sand Man, then he would be summoned by the Vortex and would be made to grant any wishes to him, Lord Zhakhan - because he was the one to bare the decanter as a gift!

Looking at the pocket watch, he decided that he should also present it as gift. Lord Zhakhan knew that he could not destroy it himself, but if the watch were to be in the hands of the Vortex, then it would be as far away as possible from Tristan's reach and then Tristan would not be able to stop time.

As he sat and continued to think, he suddenly started to hear music playing throughout his fortress.

Where was this music coming from? What kind of magic had brought sweet music to his fortress?

What was the beauty that Mariella had seen and how had this beauty managed to enter into his land of darkness? This was a very big mystery and a very big problem to him, as he was not used to anyone challenging him - especially not in his own fortress.

As he sat there, his thoughts centered on the powers of the Vortex. He knew that once all of the clocks were placed into the swamp, they could not be destroyed unless he could decipher the code or unless he could reach the centre of the Vortex and then cast his spells at the final chime of the fifth hour.

He suddenly realised that the beauty that Mariella must have foreseen, was the beauty of Zeneka Island before it was destroyed.

But how could this be? Aah! He thought, these children must somehow know that the Vortex will neutralise the swamp back into water, so the only beauty that they could possibly be able to see was the beauty that was coming from within their souls.

Lord Zhakhan rose quickly from his chair and walked towards the potions cabinet and took out his spells of fire and darkness, so that he could prepare them to use in the Vortex.

It was all now very clear to him how he was going to challenge the children.

He knew that today was his one and only chance to be the ultimate ruler of Zeneka and because he had waited so long for this day to come, it was so important to make sure that nothing could go wrong.

So, he set to work on his plans and his evil mind could think of nothing else but winning. He had to make sure that nothing and no-one was going to stand in his way!

~ Chapter VI ~

The Forgotten Children

$\mathcal{M}$eanwhile, the children were taken down to the dungeons at the back of the fortress and thrown into a place called the Time Chambers.

'Finish these clocks!' ordered a man, and then he shut the door behind him.

In this room, the children could see hundreds of other little boys and girls, working in what looked like a machinery room. They were making and assembling clocks almost as if they were all in a trance, working in a clockwise motion, one after the other.

'How did they all end up here?' asked Eva sadly.

'Lord Zhakhan has been searching for our mother Amia for a long time because he wants the Green Monkey,' replied Kavi. 'But when he could not find her, he released more Zielers into all of the waters of the world to try to find her, but because it hasn't worked so far, any child that did enter the water, he captured.'

'The prophecy states that only the Children of Time can battle against him, so that is why he has captured as many children as he could, in case they were the ones. Then he put the memory spell over them so that they could not stand in the way of his plans to rule the world. When he realised that these children were not the chosen ones, he trapped them anyway and turned them into his slaves, and he is now making them finish the clocks so that he can destroy time at sunset,' continued Kavi.

'And he also realised that he could not force any child to come to him and that is why he has worked harder to make sure that the memory spell was more powerful, so that he could trick any child into the water in order to trap them,' added Shrina.

'So have all these children been trapped here for a year?' asked Tristan, quite shocked.

'Yes and no,' replied Shrina. 'But spells can be broken, so yes, while they are all under the memory spell, they have been trapped in this world for about a year now, but they are not yet missing from your world. I know this may sound crazy and it may not make any sense to you - but time is of the essence and without time, the world simply cannot survive, so we must break the spell of the curse today and we must defeat Lord Zhakhan, or the entire world will be lost forever!'

'When I was born, my parents gave me my name Shrina. My name means, that I have 'The Power of the Night'. In India, when most children are born, they are given a name which kind of symbolises their personality and the type of person they will grow up to be. I have been blessed and protected by the shadows of the night. What this means, is that I have been given a special power that enables me to call upon them to protect us, should we require their help,' she continued.

'And my name Kavi means, that I am a 'Son of Rhyme',' Kavi broke in. 'What this means is that in India, it is very common for people to pray either in a form of a song or by rhyme. When we were born, and because we were twins, mother and father were so happy to be gifted with two children in the same month of India's holy prayer season. It is not very common to be a twin in India, so they believed that they had been blessed by the gods to bare one girl and one boy on the same day.'

'Shrina was born exactly at midnight and I came just minutes later, which is why they named her the Power of the Night. Just as I was born, because mother and father are royalty, the music started playing to rejoice the birth of twins and that is how I became the Son of Rhyme,' explained Kavi.

'That sounds wonderful, I wonder if our names have beautiful meanings like yours do,' said Mariella.

'I believe that your name Mariella, means 'Star of the Sea'. This means that your personality flairs with kindness, adventure and grace,' replied Kavi.

'Oh, that's lovely, I love it. 'Star of the Sea!'' shouted out Mariella. 'I feel like I should be a mermaid or something, I absolutely love it!'

'What does my name Evangelina mean?' asked Eva.

'Your name Evangelina, means happiness,' replied Kavi. 'Your personality is pure and honest and the meaning behind your name is 'Good News'.'

'Wow!' said Eva, shocked. 'That's really strange how a person can actually grow up and adapt to the meaning of their name. I am an honest person and you're right about the term 'good news', because that is all I have ever wanted in life for everyone.'

'This is well exciting, what does *my* name mean, Kavi?' asked Tristan.

'The name Tristan, means 'A Valiant Knight',' replied Kavi. 'Your personality shines through with courage and strength and the nature of your personality makes you a born winner!'

'That's absolutely wicked!' shouted Tristan. 'A Valiant Knight!' I just hope that my strength and courage shines through when we face the Vortex later, and I hope that we will *all* be winners soon.'

'And what does my name mean, Kavi?' asked Isaac, also feeling intrigued.

'I believe your personality makes you a fearless adventurer and a person of strong will, Isaac. The meaning behind your name is, 'He will laugh',' said Kavi.

'That's awesome! I am a fearless adventurer and as for its meaning, I do intend to laugh when we beat that wretched uncle of yours later,' said Isaac, making everyone burst into laughter.

'So, between the six of us,' said Tristan, 'we have the powers of the night, which will help us if we need them, then we have the master of rhyme, who can chant against Lord Zhakhan and now we also have a star of the sea, a bearer of good news, the one who will laugh last and the one who has the courage and strength of a knight! What more do we need? Now, all we have to do is just keep believing in ourselves and together we can achieve anything!'

'Yes, Tristan you are absolutely right,' replied Shrina. 'Lord Zhakhan is not afraid of any of us because we are children, but he does not know our strengths, so we must keep believing in ourselves, and now that you have brought the gifts that will be required in the Vortex, all we have to do is stay true to ourselves and only then, will we be strong enough to face our challenge ahead.'

'But Lord Zhakhan has taken most of the objects,' said Isaac.

'Don't worry, it doesn't matter about that,' said Kavi. 'The prophecy has called for these items and as long as they get into the Vortex, either through us or by my uncle, that is all that's required, because without them, no-one, including Uncle Zhakhan, can enter into the Vortex and I think he knows that, too!'

'I have an idea to make Uncle Zhakhan feel worried about facing us,' said Shrina. 'Mariella, do you still have your flute?'

'Yes, here it is,' replied Mariella, taking out the silver flute from her pocket.

Shrina then stepped into the middle of the room and began to chant:

'SHADOWS OF THE NIGHT, ALL RISE AND FLAIR
TRAVEL FAST, SEND MUSIC THROUGH THE AIR
TRAVEL THROUGH THE TUNNELS
TRAVEL THROUGH THE WALLS
LET THE MUSIC WHICH PLAYS, BE HEARD BY
ALL!'

'Mariella, play a song, play any song that you know,' said Shrina.

As Mariella played a beautiful song, everyone could feel the walls and the ground gently shaking around them and then, from nowhere, they could see dark mists emerging from the floor, the ceiling and the walls. Loud swishing noises started to erupt and the room began to fill up with silvery silhouettes flying around and circling above them.

'Whoa! They are so beautiful!' shouted Tristan and Isaac together.

They could see a vision of many beautiful young girls floating through the air. A cool breeze could be felt by their flowing silvery capes, and as they drew nearer, their glittery faces were so fair and pure, that they looked as if they were like real angels.

They had beautiful long hair; some had brown hair, some had black hair and some had golden coloured hair. Each girl had pretty flowered rosettes entwined neatly upon her head, displaying flowers that were made up of so many colours.

The children just stared in amazement as the vision around them was really quite mesmerising.

'My fair shadows,' said Shrina. 'As you glide upon your travels, echo this sweet music through the fortress and let the sounds be heard by all.'

As Mariella continued to play, the silhouettes started to disappear through the walls, taking the music with them. The echoes of the song could be heard by all through the tunnels, and it got louder and louder as it travelled.

As Mariella finished playing her song, as if by magic, the song continued to play on and on, just as Shrina had requested.

'Whoa! That's really cool!' shouted Isaac.

'Excellent! Now that should really confuse your uncle!' laughed Tristan.

'Luckily, his men didn't search us because I still have the kaleidoscope,' said Isaac smugly.

'Yes, and I still have my flute,' added Mariella.

'But we gave the other things away, so we can't use them, can we?' asked Eva.

'You were very brave to do that, but who is the Sand Man?' asked Shrina.

'I made him up,' replied Eva. 'I saw how brave Isaac was to speak up to Lord Zhakhan and I suddenly remembered that I had a dream of some kind which involved the Sand Man, so I thought that if I invented a leader, then it might have helped us somehow.'

'Well, you were all very clever to do what you did!' said Kavi. 'Lord Zhakhan will not know how to use your things, so we will have to try and think of a way to get them back.'

The children looked around the huge room where they could see all the other children working hard, making so many clocks.

'How can we free them from their trance?' asked Tristan.

'The only way that we can free them is by breaking the curse before sunset,' said Kavi.

'Yes,' added Shrina. 'We were separated from them a long time ago, so we could not use our powers to help them get to the Fountain of Innocence in time, but if we can break the code of the Vortex, then their trances will be broken.'

'Well then, that's what we will have to do!' said Isaac. 'We're all in this together and as a team, we will beat Lord Zhakhan!'

'Yes, we will!' shouted the others.

Tristan, Isaac, Mariella, Eva, Shrina and Kavi then hurried to join the other children to get the last of the clocks finished.

As everyone began rushing around, Kavi recited:

'GODS OF SONG, POETRY AND RHYME
WE ARE YOUR SONS AND DAUGHTER'S OF TIME
I PRAY WHEN TIME COLLIDES AS ONE
LET ALL FADED MEMORIES BECOME UNDONE'

'That's it,' shouted Isaac. 'I am now starting to remember a few things! The scroll, Tristan, the

Professor gave us that scroll. We are all supposed to be on an adventure to find… The Green Monkey! That's it! We are the ones who have been chosen to help Shrina and Kavi, quickly get it out and read it!'

Tristan took out the scroll and began to read it out loud and as they all listened carefully, they tried to make sense of the items that they had been given so that they could work out the riddle.

Tristan shouted out the riddle of the scroll for everyone to hear:

'TIME TAKES BUT ONLY TIME
MELODY PLAYS BUT ONLY IN CHIMES
NEVER SEEN AS IT SHOULD APPEAR
NEVER SEEN NOT ALWAYS CLEAR
EVER THE CURSE SHOULD IT BECOME UNDONE
ALLOWS THE COLOURS TO UNITE AS ONE'

'You're right Isaac!' squealed Mariella. 'The Professor gave us our items so that we could use our knowledge to find the Green Monkey!'

'Yes!' added Eva. 'We went looking in the manor first didn't we but then we became distracted by the lights that were in Crystal Water Lake!'

'Oh yeah,' said Tristan, pulling out a piece of paper from his pocket. 'The last thing that the Professor gave us was this note when we were in the Hall of Treasures and it says':

'*Remember, with great knowledge, comes great power!* '

Mariella then remembered the inscriptions that they had seen on the walls of the hall and started to recite the words out loud:

**'TIME IS OF THE ESSENCE
LIFE IS A RAINBOW FULL OF DREAMS
FORTUNE FAVOURS ONLY THE BRAVE'**

'The Professor told us that we only had until the final chime of the fifth hour to complete our quest and this is what he must have meant,' said Mariella.

'Yes, and although we don't have much time, I think that *this* was meant to be our adventure all along!' added Eva.

'Yeah, and he said that he had picked us from the best of the best and I know he believes in us, so we must now be brave and solve this quest, because if we do, then we might even find the Green Monkey!' said Isaac.

They all began to think about the adventure that lay ahead of them. Working away as fast as they could, they joined the other children to assemble the clocks.

Lord Zhakhan had ordered that the clocks were not to have any hands on any of the dials and that no clock whatsoever was to make any ticking noises, this was to make sure that no-one could possibly tell what time it was!

'These clocks do not show what time it is, so how are we going to know when it's sunset?' asked Mariella.

'Don't worry, once we have finished the clocks, I think that Lord Zhakhan's men will come and get us because he will not allow anything to go wrong today,' replied Kavi.

'We must be careful from now on though, because he will now be able to hear the music playing through the walls and in the tunnels, so he is going to be very angry and he will now be looking everywhere, including in here to find out where that music is coming from, so make sure you keep the flute hidden, Mariella,' said Shrina.

'So, these clocks we are making, why are they *all* going to be destroyed?' asked Isaac.

'I'll explain that,' said Shrina. 'All these children have been captured from somewhere all over the world, so they have now potentially become the hands of time. What this means is that whilst they are under a trance, time that has been turning all over the world, can now be destroyed because these children have had their memories faded and, therefore, they cannot tell anyone about what lies ahead. The sad thing is that they are helping to destroy the whole world, but they do not even know that they are doing it!'

'Oh, now I see! So Lord Zhakhan needs to stop time because then there will be no need for a prophecy to exist every hundred years and that means that good can then no longer have any chances to oppose evil. So, if he wins against the Vortex, then no-one, except for us, will know how he did it - so that means that no-one will be able to challenge him ever again, am I right?' said Tristan.

'Yes, that's right, Tristan.' replied Shrina. 'So that is why they have been given the name as - The Forgotten Children. If Lord Zhakhan does win, then the whole world will be taken over and his crimes, will too, be forgotten forever.'

'Oh, so when you told us that the children had been captured, they have actually been caught between two worlds. At the moment they are not actually missing from their world yet, but here on the island they have been trapped for about a year and if we do not break the code, then they will be lost forever, is that right?' said Eva.

'Yes, it is their soul that has been captured,' replied Shrina sadly. 'And if we don't beat him, then our mother and father will be banished forever and we too will all end up being slaves to Uncle Zhakhan.'

'Is that why your clothes are made of old cloths, so that you and Kavi do not look like royalty anymore?' asked Mariella, feeling sad for them.

'Yes, we have been made to dress as slaves,' replied Shrina modestly.

'Well, we have been sent here for a reason, so we will not let him win!' said Tristan reassuringly.

'Your uncle and his Gunda's have destroyed your beautiful island for too long now and we are going to help you to get it back, and then your mother and father will be free,' added Isaac boldly.

'Tell us about the Vortex. What will we have to do there?' asked Eva.

'The Vortex rises every hundred years but only on the last day of the century,' explained Kavi. 'It is encrypted with letters and those who dare to try and cross it will have to break its code. It's not easy, as the Vortex is very powerful and its path can change at any time. Many have tried to break the code but no-one has ever succeeded.'

'But, why is there a Vortex?' asked Isaac.

'The Vortex was created many many centuries ago. The main reason as to why it exists, is so that it can protect the Earths of the World. For many centuries now, mankind has always been in battle for money and power and when the Vortex arose, its sole purpose was to be the ultimate challenge between good and evil. The Vortex is a test for any person who dares to enter its ground. That person must prove that they are worthy to take on such a dangerous challenge,' answered Kavi.

'What has happened to those people who have failed to break the code? And what if they were good people?' asked Isaac, very curiously.

'The Vortex is very powerful. When a person has entered into the challenge, the Vortex is able to tell if that person's soul is worthy or not. Even if the code has not been deciphered by sunset, the Vortex can still sense if a person is good or not, and if they are good then they will be removed from the Vortex grid and will be returned back to their land.'

'And if a person is bad?' quizzed Isaac.

'Those who are not worthy will disappear and be banished into the earth's atmosphere, which is a never-ending black hole,' replied Kavi.

'So, how will Lord Zhakhan be able to beat the Vortex?' asked Tristan.

'He can't! His intentions are to sacrifice 'The Children of Time'. He wants to destroy all of the clocks, because if he can do that by sunset - then the encryption of the Vortex's code will just explode. He is a very clever man, and he knows that if time is destroyed, then the Vortex will never ever be able to rise again!' replied Kavi.

'What a cowardly man he is!' shouted Isaac.

'Oh, and how wicked!' added Mariella.

'Aah! So, as we are now the Children of Time, he wants *us* to disappear because he thinks that we have brought powers with us that may be able to challenge him, is that right?' asked Eva.

'Yes, and because the Vortex must be crossed by all, including Lord Zhakhan, he thinks that your powers will help him to break the code, so when he crosses the Vortex - he will intend to follow our every move,' explained Kavi.

The noises inside the large three-tiered room started to get louder and louder, as more and more clocks were slowly being completed. The clocks could be seen travelling along a long, windy and very noisy conveyor belt.

The children could not believe their eyes - there were so many clocks of all different sizes that had already been assembled, right in front of their eyes.

'Tell us about the Professor,' said Shrina. 'Who is he and what kind of adventure are you supposed to be on?'

'We call him Professor, but his real name is Patrick Joseph Michael Dowley,' said Eva. 'He is a wonderful, wonderful man! He is so famous and he is a lecturer and he is also a very famous author, too. He owns a beautiful manor in the Lake District, but for some reason, I can't remember what he named his manor.'

'Well, anyway, the manor is massive and it's so beautifully decorated inside and it is near to Crystal Water Lake, which is where we were... when we got caught by the Zielers. He writes so many novels and not only does he do that, he has also collected so many gifts from around the world. He has also generously opened his manor as a tourist attraction so that everyone can visit there to see his wonderful things.'

'Yes, and there's more,' continued Tristan. 'His manor has the most awesome looking entrance, which is designed like a chess board and it looks absolutely brilliant. Just recently, he arranged a children's writing competition and we are the four lucky winners that he picked. Our quest is to take part in an adventure from a new book that he has just written, but funnily enough, I just can't remember the name of it right now, but if it does come back to me, I'll let you know.'

'Yeah, that's right, Tristan,' said Isaac. 'We were on an adventure to find a green monkey! We were only given this scroll which is full of riddles, and our own items, and we were supposed to be working out the clues to find it, but we were told that we had to find it before the final chime of the fifth hour or I guess we would have lost the game.'

Isaac began to feel slightly strange and he started to scratch his head, whilst slowly remembering a few more things to add on to the others' conversation.

'Keep thinking,' said Kavi. 'I think the curse of Goola Bala Swamp is now slowly starting to wear away from you. Just keep trying to think of anything that you can remember.'

'The Professor gave us these items but we didn't even start our adventure, so I'm really not sure what we have to do with them. I can remember us all racing in and out of the manor looking for clues, but that's all we did. We then saw some lights by the lake, when suddenly - we all just ended up here!' said Mariella.

'Wait a minute,' said Eva. 'Isn't this all a bit strange? I mean we were all on a quest to find a green monkey and then we were told that we had to find it before the final chime of the fifth hour and we were given these items, which none of us knew what to do with, and now we have ended up here and it seems as though our adventure is somehow linked to Zeneka Island!'

'Think about it, our items have been called upon to be used here, and we are the ones who have been called upon to use them. The Professor's exact words were - '*only when clear can it be used to protect you!*' That's it! We *are* the Children of Time! Don't you remember, at the very beginning, the Professor congratulated us for being the winners and then he specifically said that we were the *chosen ones*?'

'Yes, that's right, Eva,' gasped the others.

'Now all we have to do is try and figure out how to use our things,' replied Eva.

'Yes, and the one thing that we have all remembered, is that we were on an adventure - and now, I'm pretty sure that this is where our adventure is about to begin!' said Tristan.

'Well Gunda's or no Gunda's, we are going to win this battle, and with us being the chosen ones, we are not going to fail this quest!' shouted Isaac, very loudly.

'At least the curse is starting to wear off now, so it shouldn't be too long before you can remember everything!' said Shrina excitedly.

'Yes, and when we do get our memories back, Lord Zhakhan had better watch out, because we are going to be ready for him!' said Tristan.

They all stopped talking and continued to work on the clocks and, as they worked, they could still hear the sweet song that Mariella had played on her flute - it was still travelling and playing quite loudly throughout the tunnels of the fortress!

The echo of the song seemed very distant and it had an eerie sound that seemed to flow endlessly further and further away.

The children knew that it was only a matter of time before Lord Zhakhan would come looking for them, so they continued to work and each child desperately started to ponder over their quest to try and think really hard about how they were going to be able to cross the dangerous Vortex.

Somehow, the soft sweet sounds of the music seemed quite relaxing and gave all of the children a feeling of peace.

One-by-one, all six of the children started to drift away into their own little dream. Shrina and Kavi drifted back to their memories of happiness before their beautiful island was invaded.

Tristan, Isaac, Mariella and Eva tried to think back to what had happened - and as they did, they slowly started to remember more and more things that they had been told by the Professor. They all began to feel a few memories slowly coming back to them.

It really did seem as if the music *was* trying to spell out a thousand words…

Just as the Professor had said so!

~ Chapter VII ~

Memory versus Memory

Closing their eyes, all of the children began to drift off into a world of their own. As they started to dream, the four children tried to visualise the Professor's riddles over and over again and Shrina and Kavi started to dream about their life before Lord Zhakhan had invaded the island.

Leading their minds to wander, the twist of all of their combined thoughts was so colourful that it seemed as if they were all combining... 'A Rainbow Full of Dreams!'

Shrina wandered back to the good old days when she and her family were living in India. She started to think about the beautiful sights and all of the lovely places that she had seen there. Her mind filled with thoughts of the many animals that roamed freely in the jungles, to then seeing the beautiful sights of the waterfalls that she lived so close to.

In her mind, she could see herself and Kavi playing with their friends in the sunshine and she could only vision daylight! Memories of her mother and father entered into her head and the feeling of love and happiness filled within her.

Her parents were the king and queen, she kept thinking, and they had achieved so many kind and wonderful things and had helped so many people, so why were they being punished?

Thoughts of their palace entered into her head as she imagined the glorious banquets and parties that had been held there.

She imagined the clothes that she had once worn, as they were beautiful Indian clothes, full of beads and glittery sequins, and she imagined herself laughing and dancing with many people.

She then thought about the wonderful prayer ceremonies that were held throughout India and she pictured the entire gods of India. Thoughts of singing, dancing and laughter filled her mind and then she saw visions of many glowing candles and fireworks exploding in the skies.

Suddenly, as she felt so happy, she remembered why they had to flee India to come to Zeneka Island, and sudden flashbacks of darkness started to appear in her head. She remembered that Lord Zhakhan had invaded their palace to look for the Green Monkey, and then he captured her father, and then suddenly her mother disappeared too.

Thoughts of sadness entered into her mind as a whirlwind of thoughts suddenly started to explode all at once. First she could see happiness, daylight and colourful views and then the next thing she could see was her evil uncle casting his spells of darkness all over the island and destroying the beauty of the whole land.

Round and round in circles her thoughts became mixed, from seeing all good things to then seeing many bad things. Her mind started to spin as she thought of her family and then she pictured many beautiful animals roaming around.

She then had thoughts of having fun and laughter and seeing bursts of colour, and then suddenly it all changed again, and the next thing she saw was just empty spaces, flames of fire and darkness!

As her mind wandered back into the Time Chambers with the other children, she looked around her and, by seeing the views of the forgotten children, she started to feel so much stronger in her mind because she knew then - that courage would be enough to save all of the children and her family.

Kavi's mind started to drift off as he began to think about being the Son of Rhyme. His memories were taking him back to the prayer ceremonies in India. He could remember being taught by his parents how to rhyme and how they taught him and Shrina the meaning of the words that were portrayed by either a song or by rhyme.

He then realised that this was a gift that was given by God, so that any person would be able to learn the lessons of life, before choosing the path that they would wish to take.

Thoughts of colourful views entered his head and he started to picture seeing the beauty of the land in Zeneka along with all of the happiness and laughter of the many people who were celebrating life whilst holding candles in their hands.

Flashbacks then began to appear in his mind, and the once seen happiness started to change into fire and darkness, and he remembered how Uncle Zhakhan had invaded the island. He pictured seeing the land of Zeneka being destroyed by fire and also how he had to watch their beautiful Zeneka Palace crumble down to the ground and be replaced by the big, ugly, grey stony fortress.

Feelings of anger came over him, but this was a good feeling because it was making him stronger!

Kavi knew that Zeneka Island belonged to his family and now the time had come for him to unite as one with Shrina and the Children of Time to save his home, his family and all of the other captured children that had suffered by the hands of his evil uncle.

He started to think back to his rhymes of prayer and, as he did, he remembered his favourite rhyme and began to recite it over and over again in his head:

'Beauty of the skies, beauty of the grounds
Life is a blend of many different sounds
The eyes of a tiger - see no fear
The strengths of an ox - should battle appear
Life is for living, life is your gold
Life has no questions, when one bares their soul
Thank you oh Lord, for the gifts we receive
Thank you oh Lord, for the courage within me'

As Kavi finished reciting his favourite prayer, he began to drift back into the Time Chambers and now it was clear to him that with the strength and courage of all of them together, they could defeat Lord Zhakhan!

Kavi was now feeling much stronger inside and now his mind was ready for battle. This day was going to be the day where good would verse evil, but in his mind this was also going to be their victorious day *and* this was going to be the day which would be remembered by all. He then set to work as he continued to think of as many plans as he could to overcome any obstacles that would be set by his uncle.

Tristan's mind started to spiral, taking him into a vision of places. His imagination led him back to a circus, full of happy people wandering about but then they suddenly disappeared right in front of him. In a haze of dust, he found himself alone, juggling circles of many colours. He could see that the colours of the circles were blending together, whilst floating away and taking him with them.

Memories of the chess board entrance to Mritsa Manor entered into his mind, taking him there whilst reminding him of the beautiful black and white room that first captured his attention at the start of his journey. His mind began to fill with memories of meeting his new friends, seeing Miss Deena, Jungle Joe and the Professor.

Flashbacks of events started whirling around him as he pictured Mritsa Manor and the Hall of

Treasures. He caught sight of the many Grand Father clocks which seemed to be everywhere. He remembered laughing and dancing with the other children, to then next seeing sudden flashes of light through the hall windows.

He felt himself spinning round and round whilst his mind started to fill up with loud noises of what seemed like a thousand clocks ticking away. He visualised a golden scroll unravelling itself, revealing large bold words that beckoned him to read its riddle.

Tristan pictured dark skies, remembering that all of the children had been running through thunder, lightning and heavy rain towards the lake. He remembered the calm waters of the lake, suddenly turning into an angry rage of waves pulling them all under. His mind still spinning, he pictured the beauty of the manor's gardens, the forests, the trees and the stony country lanes.

Tristan's thoughts started to rush through him all at once. He imagined that he was running through the manor. Room to room, all he could see was ticking clocks and flashes of light to then seeing thunder, lightning and rain falling everywhere. He felt as if his mind was about to explode with thoughts, but he captured everything that seemed to be coming back to him.

As if he were now in a whirlwind, he felt himself spinning round and round in bright lights, before falling into gushing water. He looked up and saw images of clocks falling from the skies above, but then suddenly everything just stopped and he found himself in complete darkness.

As his mind stopped dreaming, he drifted back to reality, back to being in the Time Chambers with the others. His last thought was a vision of an exquisite large black and white clock which was on top of the manor. Many thoughts churned around in his head, but now he could remember everything!

As he thought about the music that they had all heard in The Hall of Treasures, he suddenly remembered the chiming of all of the clocks in the manor. Then, he could remember hearing the words -

"It's always best to keep time on your side!"

Now he knew why the Professor had given him the pocket watch!

Isaac's mind wandered off, taking him to a Funfair. Thoughts of carousels, clowns, coconut stalls and other funfair games entered his head. He then saw a vision of many different coloured balloons floating away in the sky above him. He felt himself jumping onto various rollercoaster rides that seemed to be taking him higher and higher and up towards the clouds.

He tried to follow the path of the balloons but he couldn't find them and then he found himself lost and trapped in a maze of mirrors.

The mirrors that had surrounded him gave him different flashbacks. He could see the faces of his new friends calling to him through the mirrors, before disappearing into his reflection. The path beneath him kept changing from one colour to another and taking him into different directions.

Feeling as though he was still on a rollercoaster ride, he found himself whizzing into the Hall of Treasures, to then seeing flashes of light, before disappearing into the gardens of Mritsa Manor.

He started to remember seeing colours all around the manor; from the mosaic floors, to next the black and white entrance of the manor and then the colourful gardens, which then led him to the beautiful clear blue lake.

Isaac then pictured being in a limousine with his friends and then he started to remember the reason why they had all gone to the manor in the first place. He thought of laughing and dancing with his friends, to then exploring the manor's gardens and playing on the shore by the lake.

He then started to picture the Professor handing him the coloured circles and the kaleidoscope and then he remembered hearing the words -

"See only what you need to see!"

His rollercoaster ride continued and his thoughts started racing as he pictured the Zielers in the water, screeching and snapping their sharp teeth all around him. He felt as though he was riding turbulently under the lake. As the ride whizzed and whooshed through the water, Isaac could feel himself entering into a wind tunnel. He felt himself zoom through the water and through the windy tunnel, seeing only flashes of colourful light before him.

He pictured thousands of balloons bursting right in front of his path. There were colours bursting absolutely everywhere around him, taking his thoughts and his journey into all kinds of different directions. Suddenly, Isaac's ride came to a grinding halt and he found himself alone in a large deserted area of open ground.

Thoughts of adventure entered into his mind and memories were drifting back. He was now beginning to remember a flashback of events. His mind started spinning as he pictured; the manor, The Hall of Treasures, his friends and his love of rollercoaster rides. Everything that his mind could see, spun round and round until it suddenly disappeared into one big flash of light.

That was it! As Isaac's mind started to drift back into the Time Chambers, his last thought was a vision of seeing so many things. He then realised, that when the time came, he would only need to see what was right there in front of him!

Mariella's mind drifted off, taking her back into The Hall of Treasures. She started to dream of all of them being at a Masquerade Ball full of people who were all so elegantly dressed up. She pictured herself wearing a sparkling gown whilst dancing and spinning around with the others. But as she twirled around the room, she found herself twirling faster and faster and her vision started to become very hazy.

Suddenly, all that she could see was the hall spinning round and round, getting faster and faster, and now she could only see many masked faces circling around her and just staring at her before disappearing into a flash of light.

Next she found herself disappearing into the gardens of the manor. Looking around, she could only see the beauty of all the flowers that were blossoming into so many colours. The garden looked so spectacular and vibrant as it glowed and its vision took her mind into a rainbow full of colours.

Mariella started to picture Miss Deena playing her sweet song, and then thoughts of music started to enter into her mind.

She could then remember hearing the Professor say -

"No-one knows what lies behind the power of music!"

She then pictured a flashback of events. She remembered all of the children writing their names in the sandy shore of the lake, and then pictured seeing the dark skies towering over the manor and over the lake.

As she thought back to the lake, she remembered seeing it light up like glowing crystals, and then she remembered seeing the watery stairway that looked as clear as glass, opening up in the lake and pulling them all in.

As her mind wandered around in circles, she remembered seeing a rainbow pattern on the floor of the hall when the sunlight had reflected on the mosaic flooring. Suddenly, as if all at once, Mariella's mind started picturing; clocks, water fountains, flowers, trees, dancing, laughter, rainbows, and orchestras of music. Thinking about the music playing, she then had flashbacks of ballerinas dancing, children laughing and only visions of beautiful surroundings.

She was now starting to remember everything!

Mariella thought about the inscriptions on the walls that she had seen in The Hall of Treasures and now she knew what the meaning behind those words were actually trying to spelling out.

Everything that she had seen was now falling into place. She remembered turning up to the manor with her friends. Everything that the children were blessed to have seen - were sights of beauty to their eyes.

As Mariella's memory returned, her mind was full of pictures that painted out a thousand words.

She pictured the manor and all of the wonderful things that were in the garden, and then she thought about all of the Professor's treasures that the children had seen and somehow, it now, all began to make sense!

She thought back to the Professor telling them about his adventures as she drifted back into The Time Chambers.

Mariella, now realised that life itself was a journey and the reality of it all, was that everyone at some point in their lives, would have to face the bad things in life as well as experiencing all of the good things!

Eva's mind drifted off into a mist of clouds. She felt herself walking alone in complete darkness through a forest of trees, and as she walked, seeing only bright lights sparkling and dazzling ahead of her - she could feel herself being drawn towards Crystal Water Lake.

The unsettled skies were of a deep purple and blue colour which contained dark black clouds that were shadowing over the lake and the mountains.

As she walked along the wet sandy shore, in her mind she could hear sweet music playing, which seemed to echo gracefully across the clear waters of the lake.

Eva pictured the sun slowly setting peacefully in the distance. A subtle mist was covering her view, but as she watched, she saw visions of silvery mists shaping into what looked like a lady floating gracefully across the lake.

As this silvery shadow flowed across the lake, the water started to glitter like a bed of crystals, making the atmosphere truly peaceful and so magical. The lake was so calm, and the soothing view of the gentle ripples of the water slowly took

Eva's mind to the water fountain at the front of Mritsa Manor.

The large magnificent fountain flowed very high with water and was bursting out with little water drops, showering Eva as she felt the water's purity cover her. She then began to remember looking out of the window and watching the beauty of the manor's gardens with the other children.

Thoughts of The Hall of Treasures took her mind back to seeing the rainbow colours of light across the floor, to then, the flash of light from the window, and then suddenly taking her and her friends into Zeneka Island.

She was reminded of the single drop of water hitting the swamp and then she remembered seeing an almighty fire track surrounding the island.

Suddenly a flashback of; circles of light, rainbows, water fountains, misty clouds, silvery shadows and a beautiful dazzle of crystals, swirled around in her head. Eva then started to remember hearing the words -

"Only when clear can it be used to protect you!"

Eva then pictured the crystal decanter that she had been given and then her mind began to fill up with thoughts of beauty, purity and serenity. As she thought about the quest of finding the Green Monkey, suddenly things became very clear to her!

As she remembered being named as 'The Visionary One', Eva then realised that the Professor's quest could only be solved, if they all worked together as one and only if they all believed in their own strengths.

She remembered seeing the words, 'only purity of the soul may walk in victory' that were written on the golden scroll, and then she realised how the crystal decanter mysteriously became full of water.

It was Miss Deena that had said that water helps to purify the soul, so it was just *clear* and pure water that was in the bottle all along - and things could only become *clear* to a person if their soul was pure!

Eva thought back to how everything about Mritsa Manor was beautiful, peaceful and seemingly so magical. That was it! She thought.

She started to remember all four of the children's short stories and as she began to combine all of their stories together in her mind, she found herself considering the thought of fantasy becoming reality.

Eva's mind drifted back into the Time Chambers and her thoughts became visions of mystical sights.

The answers were right in front of them - all along!

Now she began to realise why the Professor had given her and her friends such wonderful gifts and how it was now so important for her and the others to use their knowledge wisely.

'Oh, now I remember the name of the Professor's book,' said Tristan. 'It's called... *The Emerald Island!*'

'Oh, so were you set on an adventure in his manor to find a green monkey?' asked Shrina.

'Not just any old monkey, Shrina, The Green Monkey - The God of Peace!' replied Isaac, sounding very shocked.

'Yes, how strange,' said Mariella, 'and we were told that we had to find it and return it to Zeneka Palace!'

'Before the final chime of the fifth hour!' added Eva. 'Oh my, his book is about this island, and our items have to be used here to help you two. He said something about Zeneka Island being better known as The Emerald Island, which is the name of his book! And now I can remember the name of his manor - it's called...'Mritsa!'

'And, oh, how bizarre! He did also mention someone called Lord Zhakhan and he also said something about a swamp!' said Mariella.

'Yes, that is very strange, isn't it?' said Shrina. 'Your quest certainly does seem very similar to the things that are going on here!'

'So what made you head for the lake in the first place, did you think that there would be clues down there for your quest in the manor?' added Kavi.

'Well, it's funny that you should say that, Kavi,' said Tristan. 'The lake had absolutely nothing to do with our adventure at all. When we first turned up at the manor, we were waiting to meet the Professor in his hall, when suddenly we saw a light flash in the window and we thought it had come from near the lake, and so we felt quite curious about it and wanted to find out if the light was coming from there.'

'Yes, and then we met a gardener called J.J. and he took us to the lake and told us some wonderful stories about the manor and about the lake,' added Mariella.

'Yeah, and then strangely enough, when we were starting our quest, it began to thunder and lightning, and then it poured down really hard with rain, and then we saw some lights coming from by the lake, so when we went down there to see what was going on, the lake... just kind of lit up!' said Isaac.

'Yes, and then the next minute we saw some steps appear in the middle of the water and we somehow kept walking towards them, and then the next minute, we were all pulled under the water by ... The Zielers!' said Eva.

'So *now* we all know how we got here!' added Isaac.

'Oh!' said Shrina, shocked. 'Yes, it does look as though your adventure is meant to be here after all, doesn't it?'

'So, it must all be true, because you have brought the items that the prophecy has sent for, but no-one could have predicted which children would have been called upon to be 'The Children of Time!'' said Kavi.

'Yes, you're right, Kavi,' said Shrina. 'You four are the chosen ones - you are the ones who have been called upon!'

The memory of all of the children had now fully returned and they continued to work hard to finish making the clocks because they all knew that the fate of the whole world now lay in their hands!

The room fell silent as the children gathered their last thoughts, and the music that had been playing, now faded away and could no longer be heard by anyone.

'Listen! The music has stopped playing,' said Shrina quietly.

'That means it must be nearing sunset,' said Kavi.

'So what happens now?' asked Tristan.

'Now we have to wait until Lord Zhakhan and his men come to get us,' replied Kavi.

'But don't let on that you all have your memories back,' added Shrina.

The last of the clocks were finally finished and the children knew that Lord Zhakhan would be coming soon, so they all started to prepare themselves to have an adventure of a lifetime!

Suddenly they could hear footsteps approaching the Chambers of Time and everyone in the room fell silent.

The doors flew open and then Lord Zhakhan and his men entered in to the room, all looking very angry.

'Who has ordered music to play throughout my kingdom?' shouted Lord Zhakhan.

'What music?' asked Shrina.

'There's no music playing,' added Kavi.

'You dare to take me as a fool? Whatever powers you think you may hold, will soon be destroyed!' boomed Lord Zhakhan.

He began to walk around the room, inspecting all of the clocks.

The clocks were all intact and finished, but the room remained silent as no-one dared to speak - and not even one of the clocks could be heard ticking!

'Take the clocks and put them all into Goola Bala Swamp. The time has now come for me to finally destroy the Vortex and rule the world!' shouted The Lord of Darkness.

Lord Zhakhan's men started to enter the room to collect all of the clocks. As the children stepped away from the machinery, Mariella made sure that she kept her flute hidden in her pocket, and out of sight.

~ Chapter VIII ~

The Vortex - Destiny of Time

$\mathcal{A}$s destiny was fast approaching its fate, Lord Zhakhan and Babagashar kept Shrina, Kavi, Tristan, Isaac, Mariella and Eva all very close by to them, and led them and all of the other children out of the fortress.

Outside was cold and dark; the skies looked painted in deep purple, with looming black clouds.

The uneasy weather towered over the whole of Zeneka Island. Holding just fire lanterns for light, everyone followed Lord Zhakhan and his men down a long track towards a deserted area of muddy ground.

The children stayed very closely together and began looking around, but nothing could be seen anywhere - it was just empty space surrounding them in the open air.

Lord Zhakhan looked up towards the sky and then raised his arms in to the air, and then started to shout out very loudly.

'Today, my fellow people, is the final day and the final hour of this sacred hundredth day. Today, my people, you will all witness my victory of power over all of mankind and on the final chime at sunset, I will conquer the Vortex and then

Zeneka Island will be mine. I will then have the power to be the ultimate ruler of the world!'

Stepping back and away from the muddy ground he then began to chant very loudly:

'RISE, OH MIGHTY VORTEX, RISE
WE AWAIT YOUR CHALLENGE
OF THE DESTINY OF TIME
HE WHO CONQUERS, SHALL CONQUER ALL
RISE, OH MIGHTY ONE, RISE FOR ALL!'

Suddenly the ground started to shake violently, knocking everyone down. The mud bubbled and fizzed as it fiercely erupted. Loud cracking noises of the ground breaking from beneath the surface, could be heard as a large stony marble hexagon-shaped grid began to arise. Everyone stood up to see a brightly lit grid starting to form whilst taking its shape across the ground.

As everyone watched in amazement, the hexagons of the grid started to flash one-by-one in different colours. More noises could be heard as the mighty Vortex used its power to make the shapes of the grid move. Slowly, each stone started to slide away from their original place before suddenly changing direction.

The power of the Vortex was so great that it looked virtually impossible for anyone to break its code!

As the Vortex stood still in completion, suddenly the mud of Goola Bala Swamp began to slowly dissolve and, as everyone watched, it started to transform back into water.

The powers of the Vortex were much stronger than the swamp and, as stated in the prophecy, Lord Zhakhan always knew that any power that dared to challenge the Vortex, could only succeed if the code could be deciphered.

Everyone watched the beautiful view of the pure water reclaiming its rightful ownership. Flowing rapidly, the gushing water diffused the fire trail that was still burning and then continued to surround the whole of the island.

The thousands of clocks that had been placed into the swamp, could now be seen by all, floating beneath the pure water - but they remained in place... for their fate!

However, the Zielers of the swamp started to dart in and out of the water, turning into flashes of light, before exploding like fireworks into the air and disappearing completely and then suddenly, there in the distance - everyone could see sunlight!

It was such a wonderful view. Far in the background of the dark skies was the vision of the sun, slowly setting and reflecting on the peaceful waters. A beautiful pale colour of orange, yellow and pink, blended tastefully into the purple skies and, as sunset was about to happen, it was time to face the final hour - it was time for the final showdown!

'It must be 4 o'clock now, that means we only have one hour to solve our quest,' whispered Tristan to the others.

'All of the clocks are now under the water except for yours, Tristan, so we must solve the code when your watch starts to chime,' said Kavi.

'And we must all be in the centre of the Vortex before the final chime,' alerted Shrina.

As the Vortex was now ready, Lord Zhakhan approached the entrance and then shouted out his pledge to the Vortex:

'Oh mighty Vortex, I enter your sacred ground and I sacrifice these gifts to you as a token of my worthiness to face your challenge.'

He then pulled out the seven coloured circles, the glass decanter and the pocket watch and laid them onto the marble stone.

The children all gasped and looked at each other, each one knowing that those objects were theirs and *not* Lord Zhakhan's!

Suddenly, a mist of smoke arose from the ground and covered the entire vision of the Vortex, but when the mist cleared, the objects that Lord Zhakhan had pledged had now disappeared completely.

The mist then re-appeared and parted into an arched shape, opening up a starting point for Lord Zhakhan to enter.

He turned around to face the children and shouted out, 'now that your powers are gone, there will be no colours to help you, there will be no mist of desire and the final clock will soon meet its destiny!' He laughed as he disappeared into the misty grid.

Inside the Vortex, Lord Zhakhan stood ready to cast his spells of darkness and then he waited for an appearance of the so-called and powerful Sand Man, but as the mist grew thicker and thicker, no-one appeared and then he suddenly realised that the children had tricked him into parting with their items.

'Fools!' he shouted. 'You dare to trick me, but your items are gone forever and now, you have no powers to use against me!' He again laughed. 'At sunset I will be the ultimate ruler of the world and everyone will bow down before me!'

The time had now come for the battle between good and evil and as the children prepared themselves to enter into the Vortex, they all turned around to look at the forgotten children that were still left standing in a hypnotic trance.

'What is going to happen to them, can we save them?' said Mariella sadly.

'Don't worry, Mariella,' replied Kavi, 'they will be safe here whilst we are in the Vortex. Shrina and I will recite one of our mother's chants to keep them protected.'

He turned to look at the forgotten children and started to chant very loudly:

'PROMISES OF ZENEKA, POWERS OF THE SAND
RETURN PEACE AND SERENITY UPON OUR LAND
CHILDREN OF TIME, JOIN HANDS AND PRAY
THAT VICTORY MAY BLESS US UPON THIS DAY!'

As Kavi finished chanting, the hundreds of forgotten children started to slowly form into many circles, surrounding Babagashar and his men, and then they all joined hands and began to pray.

Shrina then quickly added to Kavi's chant:

'SHADOWS OF THE NIGHT
PLEASE RISE - PLEASE BLESS
PROTECT OUR CHILDREN
FROM THE EVIL FORCES OF DARKNESS!'

Suddenly, the silvery silhouettes appeared again from nowhere and started to circle and float above the forgotten children, forming into a magical and colourful wisp of air.

They floated gracefully around the children, protecting them all within the circle. This powerful circle then trapped Babagashar and his men inside.

'What do we do now?' asked Tristan.

'The Vortex has neutralised the land, so we have now protected the children and our land, and now we have to bare gifts to the Vortex to show that we too are worthy to face its challenge,' replied Kavi.

'Take off the bands from your wrists, as we must now enter the Vortex baring only our pure souls. We will offer the bands as a gift,' said Shrina.

All of the children removed their wrist bands and then approached the Vortex one after the other and placed them down onto the marble stone.

'What about Isaac's kaleidoscope and my flute?' asked Mariella.

'Follow me, I have an idea!' said Isaac, taking off his shoes. 'But first you must take off your shoes, because we are about to enter sacred ground.'

Tristan, Mariella and Eva took off their shoes immediately and followed Isaac to the front of the Vortex, and Shrina and Kavi followed behind.

In Isaac's head he could now clearly hear the voice of the Professor saying:

"See what you must see, but only what you need to see!"

'Oh mighty Vortex, here we stand upon your sacred ground as The Children of Time. We bare our innocence, and we are here to offer the purity of our souls. I am the eye of the beholder and with this kaleidoscope, I ask only of you to grant me the permission to keep it,' pledged Isaac.

He then turned to Mariella. 'You must show and offer the flute as a gift so that we are given a chance to prove that we do not mean any harm.'

Mariella then took out her flute and placed it onto the marble stone along with the bands and the kaleidoscope. She too, could now also hear the Professor's voice saying:

"Music can spell out a thousand words!"

'Oh mighty Vortex, I offer you this flute as a token of peace. I ask only of you to allow melody to play. This flute bares only sweet music, which will only allow time to play in chimes,' she pledged.

As they placed the items onto the stone, they stepped back and watched as the mists zapped away the bands - but the mists did not take the flute or the kaleidoscope!

Suddenly, a sweet sound from the flute started to play from the ground of the Vortex and then it suddenly stopped. The mist formed once again into an arched shape to allow all of the children to enter in to the grid.

'I know exactly what we have to do!' shouted Isaac excitedly. 'The stones are going to keep changing directions and they will also keep changing into different colours, so we have to follow the colour patterns of a rainbow. Just keep remembering that life is a Rainbow Full of Dreams!'

'Yes, you're right Isaac,' shouted Tristan, remembering the Professor's phrase:

"Memory will serve you well!"

'We must all take it in turns to step on a stone of each colour and we must remember each letter that will appear on the stone beneath us!' said Tristan.

'Yes, and your kaleidoscope will help you to track the colours, Isaac,' shouted Kavi.

'And once we have followed the patterns correctly, the path will lead us into the centre of the Vortex,' added Shrina.

'But what about Lord Zhakhan?' asked Eva.

'He will be moving around in the grid so we must try to avoid stepping into his path!' said Kavi.

'Isaac, you go first as you will be our eyes, then it should be Shrina, Mariella and Eva, followed by Kavi, and I will go last. Okay?' said Tristan.

'Be careful, everyone, as we will lose each other as the stones move,' warned Shrina.

Isaac picked up the kaleidoscope and entered into the cloudy grid. As he disappeared from sight, he could not see clearly in front of him as it was so misty. He felt an almighty breeze fall upon him, which was coming from the windy suctions from the stone beneath him.

He kept completely still and started to look at the colours of the grid through the kaleidoscope.

Isaac knew that he did not have much time as if he did not move quickly, then the stone he was standing on would change colour and he would not be able to trace the next stone. Thinking quickly, he thought about the colours of the rainbow and he knew that he had to follow the correct colours as he had seen in The Hall of Treasures.

He stood there bravely and started to shout loudly, reciting the colours of the rainbow:

'RED! YELLOW! PINK! GREEN! ORANGE! PURPLE! BLUE!'

As he stood waiting patiently for something to happen, suddenly from above he could hear music playing. The stones started to flash into many colours and as he looked down at the grid, he could see all different letters of the alphabet appearing, but they were only on certain stones.

As the music continued to play, it seemed as though it was prompting him to search for the code.

Not knowing whether to move or not, thinking very quickly, Isaac shouted out the colour 'RED!'

He then looked through the kaleidoscope and saw a stone flashing red and he leapt onto it and stood very still.

Looking down, he could not see any letter on the stone, so bravely he jumped from red stone to red stone until, finally, he could see a stone with a letter on it!

He quickly jumped on the red-coloured stone and stood very still because he knew that the colours of the stones were about to change.

He looked down and saw the letter D imprinted on the stone below him and after remembering it, he called out as loudly as he could to the others.

'I am on the red stone, Shrina, when you enter the grid, make sure you wait until I shout yellow and then keep jumping on every single yellow stone until you find the one that has a letter on it. Okay?' he said, as he continued to shout.

'And then stay on that stone and shout out the colour that you are standing on, so that we can all hear each other. It is very noisy and windy in here and the stones are very wobbly, but make sure that you remember the letter that you have seen and then be ready to move very quickly because the colours will change!' he bellowed.

Shrina entered into the noisy grid and waited to hear the word 'yellow'. The stones started to change to a yellow colour, but as Isaac remained still, the stone that he was standing on remained as the colour red.

Thinking back to the Professor's words:

"See what you must see, but only what you need to see, especially if you find that colours try to change your path!"

Isaac suddenly realised that if the right letter is stood upon then his path would not change!

Feeling very excited and happy about being right about his idea, he quickly called out 'YELLOW' to Shrina and then shouted out to her as she took her place on a yellow stone.

'Shrina, when you find the stone with a letter on it, do not move off that stone okay, because the kaleidoscope will guide us once we are all in here,' he shouted. 'Our path cannot change as long as we stick to the correct colour code of the rainbow, okay?'

Shrina shouted back to Isaac to let him know that she had heard him, and then jumped from stone-to-stone to find the next letter. Then, looking below her, she remembered the letter of that stone, and then shouted out, 'YELLOW' and then called out to Mariella to repeat what Isaac had just instructed.

Mariella quickly picked up the flute from the floor and entered the grid and then waited for Isaac to call out the next colour. When she heard the next colour being called, she too moved quickly and then shouted out, 'PINK'.

Then Eva waited to move and by following the same instructions, she shouted out, 'GREEN'.

Kavi followed after Eva and waited to move and then he called out, 'ORANGE'.

Finally Tristan entered into the grid and waited to move and as he found his last stone, he called out, 'PURPLE'.

Just then a thought about the seven colours of the rainbow entered his head. He quickly shouted out to the others, 'don't tread on any stone that is blue! There are only six of us and that means Lord Zhakhan is following our pattern, so he must be on the colour blue! I repeat, do not tread on any of the colours that are blue, can you all hear me?'

Luckily, the others could all hear him and called out to acknowledge him. The stones began to change into the colour blue, but, as strictly ordered, no-one moved from their spot!

Suddenly, Lord Zhakhan appeared in sight on a blue stone but he did not know what to do, so he frantically jumped from blue stone to blue stone to try and catch one of the children, but the stones kept moving and he was being drawn further and further away from any of the stones that the children were standing on.

He then realised that he had no choice other than to wait on the stone that he stood upon.

The Vortex then repeated the same pattern again 4 times, but the children just continued to collect all of the letters that they needed by following the path shown by the guidance of Isaac and his kaleidoscope.

As they all continued to collect more and more letters from the stones, the Vortex started to shake and the stones below them all began to continuously change colours and then get smaller and smaller, making it harder for them to keep their balance.

But as the shaking came to an end, they all remained still and found themselves standing away from each other in the form of a circle, and Lord Zhakhan also appeared, but he was on the final blue stone facing Kavi.

There in the middle of the ground were the seven coloured circles that Lord Zhakhan had pledged earlier, but these circles were now neatly set out on the floor and were placed in front of each player with the colour of the circle matching the colour of the stone that they were each standing on.

Lord Zhakhan became very angry and then began to chant very loudly:

'Agun Baba, Jhollo! Jhollo!' (Oh Father Of Fire, Come Alive! Come Alive!)

As he shouted, a flame of fire started rising into the middle of their circle and the grid became hotter and hotter.

Shrina then quickly began to chant:

'POWERS OF THE NIGHT ALL RISE AND FLARE
PROTECT US OH LORDS OF EARTH, FIRE, WATER
AND AIR
COLOURS OF THE VORTEX UNITE AS ONE
LET BEAUTY SURPASS ALL EVIL THAT HAS
BEEN DONE!'

As Shrina finished chanting, the Vortex began to crack and the whole ground shook turbulently, throwing everyone to the floor. Suddenly, a gusty wind rose and soared through the sky, causing thunder and lightning to follow. Hard rain began to pour, flooding the fire and the Vortex, forcing Lord Zhakhan and the children into high waters.

As the fire diffused, all of the seven coloured circles that were on the floor, smashed into tiny little pieces and then transformed into a mist of coloured smoke, and the music that had been playing quite randomly - suddenly just stopped!

As the children swam to safety, they looked up to see that the smoke had now transformed into a rainbow before bursting into a beautiful shower of colourful glitter falling upon everyone, and then the dark skies lit up like sparkling diamonds. A large explosion suddenly erupted, and then everything went deadly silent!

They all stood up, facing Lord Zhakhan in the centre of the Vortex.

Suddenly four black coloured walls started to emerge from the floor blocking them all into a square shaped room. From the centre of the floor a metal vault began to rise, showing all of the letters of the alphabet upon it, and there on the floor lay the glass decanter and the pocket watch!

Lord Zhakhan moved quickly and grabbed the pocket watch and Eva quickly grabbed the glass decanter.

Head to head in silence, they stood against Lord Zhakhan, each child prepared for the final showdown!

'So, I see that you have all tried to trick me and I believe that none of you have ever possessed any powers, have you? But I can see that you have worked out the code for the Vortex, give it to me and then I may feel generous and let you all live!' boomed Lord Zhakhan.

'Never!' shouted out all of the children together.

Suddenly, Tristan's pocket watch began to chime and, as it reached the fourth chime, he suddenly remembered the Professor's wise words:

"Remember that it is always best to keep time on your side!"

Tristan stood very tall and then boldly recited:

'TIME WAITS FOR NO-ONE…
UNLESS IT IS ASKED TO DO SO!'

'OH MIGHTY VORTEX, AS THE MASTER OF TIME
I RESPECTFULLY ASK OF YOU TO CEASE
ON THIS FOURTH CHIME
A SINGLE SECOND IS OUR ONLY REQUEST
TO GIVE US TIME TO COMPLETE OUR QUEST'

Suddenly, the whole room became silent and the pocket watch stopped chiming, but as Lord Zhakhan was still holding the watch - as time stopped, he too froze on the spot!

The children ran up to the vault and by quickly remembering all of the letters that they had seen, they pressed the buttons one-by-one, spelling out:

'**DESTINY LIES UPON GOOD EARTH**'

As they tapped in all of the letters, the vault started to open up and inside of it was an inscription which gave further instructions for the final part of the code.

ENTER CODE:

Tristan quickly took out the scroll and read it out loudly. It all now made sense and the children became very excited. Tristan, Isaac, Mariella, Eva, Shrina and Kavi all held hands and looked at each other, smiling. Then altogether, they looked straight at Lord Zhakhan and then shouted out:

'Here we all stand upon Good Earth - the code is':

'MRITSA'

'There are six of us so each of us should tap in a letter of Mritsa and then Tristan you must release time so that Lord Zhakhan's curse is broken at sunset, okay?' said Kavi.

They all took turns to press in the letters of the word Mritsa, and before Tristan pressed in the last letter, he called out: 'Time is of the Essence - Time of the world, you are now free to keep turning!'

As he pressed in the last letter, which was the letter A, he quickly shouted out to Mariella, 'no-one knows what lies behind the power of music - play, Mariella!'

Taking out the flute, Mariella started to play a familiar tune that suddenly came to her. It was the same song that Miss Deena had played and as Mariella started to play the song, loud chimes could be heard by all.

Her song could be heard by all of the clocks around the world, and this sweet tune made the entire clocks chime together as one, as if they were accompanying *her* song!

Shrina and Kavi looked excitedly at each other and smiled. 'That's mother's song!' they whispered.

As the sweet tune echoed across the air, the fifth chime of Tristan's pocket watch was now free to chime alongside all of the clocks of the world!

Lord Zhakhan became unfrozen and then fell down to his knees on to the floor. The children stepped back and watched as the Vortex began to glow. The code had been broken and the curse of Goola Bala Swamp had finally been beaten!

Suddenly a whirlwind arose from beneath Lord Zhakhan and trapped him into its spiral.

As the children stood back to watch, they all shouted out to him;

'Fortune Favours Only The Brave - Only Purity Of The Soul May Walk In Victory!'

Lord Zhakhan was then zapped away by the Vortex.

The children felt themselves also being caught into the whirlwind but as they looked around, they found themselves being returned to where they had left the forgotten children.

The silvery silhouettes began to disappear as the whirlwind continued to spiral towards Babagashar and the other men, and then they too were zapped away with Lord Zhakhan - all of them banished into a black hole.

The whirlwind came to an end and the children could hear faint voices of Lord Zhakhan and his men shouting and cursing before disappearing completely.

Everyone started hugging and cheering loudly as the curse of Goola Bala Swamp was finally broken, which then also released the captured souls of the forgotten children.

The Vortex began to disappear back beneath the ground and, as the children stood watching, all around them they could see that the island was starting to change appearance right before their eyes!

The colour of the water turned back in to a crystal blue colour, the once muddy ground changed back into golden sand, and then patches of green grass started to appear.

From nowhere wild animals started to roam around, beautiful flowers bloomed and blossomed everywhere and many trees once again stood tall.

Then the most wonderful thing happened. The children saw that the stony grey fortress started to crumble and then crash down to the ground and, as they watched in excitement, in its place formed a beautiful white and pale green palace, made purely out of marble and then they could see beautiful waterfalls starting to flow either side of the palace.

Everyone stared in absolute amazement, but the magic was far from over! Suddenly the clothes of rags that each of the forgotten children were wearing, suddenly transformed back into the clothes of their native country, and now everyone was all dressed up, looking so elegant and smart.

The outfits of the world were fantastic and everyone looked so bright, colourful and truly amazing!

Shrina's clothes started to change from rags into a green velvet gown embroidered with silver sequins, and a sparkling tiara of coloured stones sat neatly upon her long shiny, black hair.

Kavi's clothes changed from rags into a smart long-sleeved shirt and trousers, which were made of black silk and his shirt, had real gold buttons down the front and then a gold band suddenly appeared upon his head.

'Wow! You two look absolutely stunning. I am so pleased that you can both now return to being royalty again,' cried Mariella, hugging them both.

As she spoke, Tristan and Isaac's clothes started to turn into smart black tuxedos with white shirts, and Mariella and Eva were now dressed in very glittery pale pink silky ball gowns and they had pretty rosettes entwined upon their hair!

Everyone danced around feeling so glamorous and as they twirled round and round, sounds of music could be heard coming from the palace.

Curiously, they stopped to look, and then saw that many people were starting to come out of the palace.

Everyone watched as the people formed into two lines, making an aisle. Suddenly, a trumpet started to play and every person began to kneel. A tall, handsome Asian man dressed in blue suddenly emerged from the palace.

His clothes were made of fine silk and a golden coloured rope was neatly tied around his waist. On top of his head was a crown bordered with real gold gems.

The whole place fell silent as he made his way through the aisle towards the children. As he walked, the water of the island could be heard swishing and swaying gently, then suddenly, as everyone turned to look at the water, it started to divide into two!

The sounds of the swishing made everyone turn around to stare towards the view of the sunset. A mist started to appear from within the water and a figure of a lady could be seen walking out onto the golden sand.

As she drew closer, everyone could quite clearly see a beautiful Asian woman dressed in a purple coloured velvet gown which was embroidered with gold sequins.

On her head was an exquisite and very expensive looking crown which sparkled and dazzled in so many coloured jewels.

Tristan, Isaac, Mariella and Eva were all shocked and just could not believe their eyes!

'Miss Deena!' they all shouted together, feeling very overwhelmed.

'Mother!' shouted Kavi.

'Father!' shouted Shrina.

Everyone now realised that the King and the Queen of Zeneka Island had now returned!

'All bow down and kneel before King Masi and Queen Masi!' shouted out a loud voice.

All of the children politely and respectfully started to kneel, as the King started to walk towards everyone.

'Please rise, my good people, the curse that once lay upon us has now been lifted and we are all free!' shouted out King Avinash, smiling.

Everyone stood back up and then started to cheer once more.

'We must all cherish this day and celebrate this glorious victory!' said King Avinash to one of his men. 'Lead everyone in to the palace and set out the banquets and let the celebrations begin!' shouted out the King.

King Avinash and Queen Amia then approached Shrina and Kavi and they all embraced one another tightly. Then Amia called over to Tristan, Isaac, Mariella and Eva and embraced them all too.

'Miss Deena, I mean Queen Amia,' said Mariella, politely correcting herself. 'But, how did this all happen?'

'Come inside and we will explain everything,' replied Amia's sweet voice.

Everyone made their way into the palace and into a very large banqueting hall. The children followed the king and queen towards a huge dining table and sat down in amazement as they watched the staff of the palace decorate the room with golden banners, balloons and long strings of beaded lights. The room looked so magnificent and was lit up so brightly, that it really did feel as though Christmas had come early!

~ Chapter IX ~

Green Monkey
The God of Peace

*O*nce everyone was seated at the many dining tables, King Avinash stood up and started to speak.

'Welcome to Zeneka Island, Everyone!'

'Our people of The Emerald Island can now all live in peace and the evil that has once dominated us has now been banished and can no longer put any of us in danger. As we all celebrate this wonderful day, I can tell you that the clocks of the world are all free and are once again turning and chiming to the times of your countries, and The Emerald Island is now free again to move under the waters of the world to protect our precious time,' said Avinash.

'We must all celebrate, that all of our prayers have been answered and that we are all safe and well. The gods of Earth, Fire, Water and Air are back in power to protect the world from being destroyed! Queen Amia and I are very grateful to all of you for helping us to save our beautiful island. Please accept our gratitude by enjoying this glorious banquet of food and drink and afterwards we shall all dance and continue to celebrate the return of peace and happiness to Zeneka,' he continued.

Everyone started to cheer as they all embraced the exciting news.

'But we have failed our quest! - We didn't find the Green Monkey,' said Tristan sadly.

Queen Amia turned to Avinash and they both started to smile at all of the children.

'No, no, you haven't failed! The Green Monkey was found when you worked together to solve the code of the Vortex! Tristan, do you still have the Professor's scroll?' asked Amia, hugging him reassuringly.

Tristan took out the scroll and handed it to the queen. Amia unravelled it and then asked Tristan, Isaac, Mariella and Eva to read out what they could now make of the riddle of the scroll.

Tristan recited, 'time takes but only time'.'

Mariella recited, 'melody plays but only in chimes.'

Eva followed with, 'never seen as it should appear - never seen, not always clear.'

And lastly, Isaac recited, 'ever the curse should it become undone, allows the colours to unite as one.'

Then Shrina and Kavi joined in and recited together.

'Only purity of the soul may walk in victory.'

'Oh, now I see! We had the answers all along but we just didn't know it!' said Tristan.

'As soon as I had the pocket watch in my hands, time was already turning and those chimes that we heard playing earlier than they should have, were playing a message for us to learn - that no matter which path we would have taken, time would only take time, so we were the only ones who could stop the danger of our tracks providing we were in the right place at the right time! And that is why the Professor said it is always best to keep time on your side. Is that right?'

'Yes, that's right, Tristan,' replied Amia. 'Time is of the essence, but in life only you can control your own destiny.'

'Melody plays but only in chimes. The Professor said that music can spell out a thousand words,' said Mariella.

'We have learned that the words of any songs do not have to have any meaning, but when music does play, it can become a memory of a person's life and their dreams, so when we found ourselves in danger, our memories took us back to familiar surroundings and then I remembered hearing your song, which then reminded us all of our strengths, and it was our own memories that remembered to spell out the letters of the words that we needed, which then helped us to break the code of the Vortex, and it was our memories, which then became a rainbow full of dreams. Is that right?'

'Yes, Mariella, but not only did your memories help you, but the fact that you all wanted to help

Shrina and Kavi regardless of knowing that you were all in danger, was the most important part of your challenge. You have all proved that you were worthy to enter the Vortex just by being willing to surrender your gifts. The Vortex is very powerful and can sense the difference between good and bad, which is why your gifts were not taken away from you,' replied Amia.

'Never seen not always clear,' said Eva. 'We all started out on a quest and we didn't know what we were looking for, but as time kept turning we found our inner strengths. We have learned that life is not always clear and not only did we meet new friends in each other, but we also found Shrina and Kavi, so it became quite clear to us in the end that it really didn't matter if we couldn't find the Green Monkey because we found time to protect each other instead.'

'When my memory started to come back, I saw a shadow of a lady in Crystal Water Lake and it made me remember that only a person's soul can be free to wander through life, and the crystal decanter that I was given was always full of water, which allowed our path to be clear right from the start. The Professor said 'only when clear could we be protected,' so as things became clearer to us, we all believed in ourselves. So that is what the inscription on the wall meant - 'Fortune Favours Only the Brave.' Is that right, Queen Amia?'

'Yes, that is right, Eva, and though your quest did not appear to be 'clear' to you all at the very beginning - eventually it did, because you were all willing to offer the purity of your souls - and that is how you all became stronger and that is also how you all managed to decipher the coloured code. Together, you worked out that even without having any powers - you could still put your strengths to the test and that is why you won,' replied Amia.

'Ever the curse should it become undone will allow the colours to unite as one,' said Isaac.

'Oh, now I see! When we were in The Hall of Treasures, the answers to the riddles of the scroll were already right in front of our eyes. So when the Professor told me to see only what I needed to see, he meant that we should only be looking for what our hearts really desired, and because we all knew that we wanted to solve the code of the Vortex and save Zeneka Island, we chose our path to save the island even if we couldn't find the Green Monkey,' he continued.

'The Professor could not tell us any more about his story because the ending of his book depended on the path that we would take and so that means... that we were his adventure all along! We did follow our hearts, so with the essence of time and by using the purity of our souls, we were then able to walk in victory! Is that right, Queen Amia?' said Isaac.

'Yes, Isaac. As you know, in all of the Professor's novels it is always curiosity that seems to lead anyone towards an adventure. He wanted you all to use your own strengths and knowledge and work together as a team to prove that any quest could be conquered, but that could only happen, if you really wanted it to, and only then would you have been able to search for the answers,' said Amia.

'The main reason as to why you cannot see the Green Monkey is because it is not always clear to look for something that you have already found.'

'Knowledge comes with great power and it was your own memories that served you well,' said King Avinash.

'By being brave you have all proved that you possessed the greatest power of all - to lift the curse that was put over the island,' he added.

Music then started to play and everyone watched as the palace staff entered the room holding silver trays of so many different kinds of food for everyone. Each table became full of many exotic foods and fruits from all over the world and it really did look like the most magnificent banquet ever seen by anyone!

The silver goblets on the tables were filled up with fresh water that had been purified from the Fountain of Innocence. Everyone closed their hands together ready to pray for the blessing of their freedom and for once again having the wonderful gift of peace and serenity.

King Avinash then raised his goblet to make a toast:

'Fountain of Innocence - in purity you flow in the Island of Zeneka, and now your beauty can once again glow. Thank you our Lord for answering our prayers. Thank you also for the good food and drink that you have blessed us all with. Our beautiful Zeneka Island is now free for all of eternity. Amen! Please commence everyone, please now enjoy your feasts.'

'Amen!' shouted everyone in the room raising their goblets to the king's toast. The room filled with happiness as everyone started to laugh and chat with each other whilst tucking into the glorious selections of food.

After the marvellous feast, the children followed the king and queen outside to the back of the palace.

The garden was lit up so brightly with hanging tea lights and lanterns, and upon the golden sand were designer green hedges with sparkling lights entwined within them.

As they followed the path, they passed many scattered trees which were also covered with lights and in so many colours. The children looked around in astonishment as the whole place felt so magical and so beautiful.

The sand was full of red rose petals which led them all towards a huge golden coloured water fountain, which was set neatly in the middle of the garden area.

The water burst out and flowed up so high, and it looked so truly amazing and they could see that embedded into the stone of the water fountain were four golden statues.

'This is the prayer garden,' explained King Avinash. 'This is our temple where we all come to pray every day to thank the gods for all of the good blessings in our lives. This is the Fountain of Innocence, and the statues that you can see are the Gods of Earth, Fire, Water and Air, who are now once again protected by purity.' He explained.

'In India, we worship many gods, but when my cousin Zhakhan invaded the country, he was mainly out to destroy the Green Monkey, our God of Peace, because the power of the Green Monkey is more powerful than mankind. The name of our treasured god is Lord Hanuman,' smiled the King.

'He is in the form of a Green Monkey and only he holds the ultimate powers of life. He has been worshipped so dearly by everyone because he is the king of adventure, strength and courage!

'He is also very wise, clever, cunning and fearless - and also by being known as a musician, his powers of music became highly religious and his strength and his will power became unbeatable, which is why Zhakhan wanted so badly to destroy him,' continued Avinash.

King Avinash then asked one of his men to get everyone from the palace to come outside.

All of the staff and the other children came outside and were handed a lit candle so that they could join in with the final prayer of the evening.

'Sons and daughters of time, as we pray on this glorious day, the curse of your memory and any lost time has now been lifted, and you are free to return to your worlds where time will keep turning, and your precious memories of life will not have been lost. The battle between good and evil has been won and once again our two worlds can collide on this glorious hundredth day. The world has been set free and you are no longer in any danger. Raise your candles as we pray to thank our God of Peace - Lord Hanuman, for allowing Zeneka Island to reign in victory!' shouted the King.

As everyone raised their candles in silence, suddenly fireworks started to flare up in to the sky and music from the palace could be heard playing loudly. The sky then filled up with sparkling colours and loud banging noises filled the air as the fireworks exploded.

As everyone watched in excitement, and looked towards the Fountain of Innocence, they could all see something appearing from within the flowing water.

It was a hologram of a statue of an emerald monkey God! It was... The Green Monkey!

Everyone gasped with pleasure as they felt so blessed to be able to witness such a rare possibility - the powerful God himself!

'We did find the Green Monkey after all! We did find Lord Hanuman, The God of Peace,' shouted Tristan, whilst feeling so excited, honoured and very emotional.

'Yes, you did, you all did!' smiled the King.

The children could not stop looking at the beautiful sight of the Green Monkey and they could not believe that they had completed their quest.

They all felt so excited, because not only did they help to save The Emerald Island, but they also found the God of Peace!

'Now I understand why it was necessary for Lord Hanuman to remain unseen,' said Tristan.

'When we started our adventure, we wanted to win the quest right from the start and in order for us to do that we had to use our own knowledge and strengths to work out the riddles. We did not know what our strengths were until we were put to the test, so we tricked Lord Zhakhan by making him think that we possessed magical powers and in a way, I guess we did - the powers of our souls!'

'So when we entered into the Vortex, it was already clear to us that we did not have to look for the answers as we had them all along, so all we really had to do was just remember everything that the Professor had told us. When we fell into the curse of Goola Bala Swamp, we all slowly started to forget about winning our quest because we thought more about survival and saving Zeneka Island, and with the help from Shrina and Kavi, we found out that by having great knowledge - came great power!' said Tristan.

'So in the end, the God of Peace was somehow with us all along and somehow, he allowed us to use his powers of adventure, courage and strength

- and that is how we managed to solve the code of the Vortex and then together, we all found peace.'

'We did not have to look for it and we did not have to see the Green Monkey either, because the purity of our souls was enough for us to eventually see that a good soul can conquer all,' he continued.

'Yes, and thinking back to when we were all in the Hall of Treasures, the Professor had different items in each of the seven coloured rooms,' said Isaac.

'The items in the red room were a symbol of adventure, energy, danger and courage. The yellow room, was a room full of wisdom, as it only contained clever looking objects that could only be used with great knowledge. The pink room had only pretty things in it, which displayed signs of love and happiness.'

'The green room was only full of peaceful items. The orange room was full of playful and creative objects and the purple and blue rooms only contained items which seemed to combine love, happiness and sorrow.'

'Yes, you're absolutely right, Isaac, because Miss Deena, I mean Queen Amia, went into the green room to get the lute to play her song,' said Mariella.

'The green room was full of paintings which were of places from all over the world. All of the pictures in there, only showed sceneries of peaceful surroundings, and all of the other items in that room including the lute, all had written descriptions of stories about each of the objects and how they were all used in a place of tranquillity. If you remember back to what J.J. had told us, he said that Queen Amia loved to paint pictures and play her songs down by the lake,' continued Mariella.

'She must have painted some of those pictures too, so that she could keep remembering her fond memories, and so that she could keep her faith of one day returning here to her family, and her song that made all of the clocks chime in The Hall of Treasures - was the right song for me to play when I was in the Vortex.'

'The song was a sign for us to know that time was running out! When I played the other song in the Time Chambers, the tune echoed through the walls to trick Lord Zhakhan into giving us enough time to finish making the clocks, so that they would work and chime along with the other clocks of the world - but only when the time was right!'

'So when I played your song in the Vortex, Queen Amia - your song of peace… did spell out a thousand words, but it only had one meaning - 'only purity of the soul may walk in victory.'

'Yes, and in the blue room, there was a mixture of objects,' said Eva. 'That room was also a type of adventure room, because it was the only room that contained objects that the Professor had collected himself over the years, and those selected items were from his own adventures.'

'The blue room was the biggest clue all along, but because we did not know what we were looking for, we completely missed seeing the most vital clue of all. When the Professor gave me the glass decanter, he specifically said that only when clear could it help us, which only now makes sense, because when a person finds themselves on an adventure, they cannot see what lies ahead of them, so nothing was ever going to be clear to us until - we experienced our own adventure!' continued Eva.

'The water in the bottle has always remained clear and pure and all we had to do was stay true to ourselves and to each other, which then finally made us see things more clearly. Everything that we saw in the manor was very colourful and very pure, but when we came here - Lord Zhakhan banished and destroyed anything that was pure and beautiful, and he kept the whole place in the dark, so that the curse of his Zielers would make it impossible for anyone to remember life as it was!'

'So every one of the rooms in the Hall of Treasures, were signs for us to see a combination of the good and the bad things in life. That is what was meant by the inscription 'Life is a Rainbow Full of Dreams.'

'Yes, and it was your courage and bravery that has brought the world back together,' said Shrina.

'There was only so much that Kavi and I could have done ourselves to protect our land, and if you didn't find the island then we may not have been able to beat Lord Zhakhan on our own.'

'Your whole adventure was like a puzzle,' added Kavi. 'Each one of us was an important piece of the puzzle, because we all shared the same dream, which was to protect Zeneka Island and to save the world from being destroyed, and even though Lord Zhakhan took your watch and the other items, we still managed to beat him.'

'Your pocket watch, the flute, the glass decanter and the kaleidoscope are all sacred items of Zeneka, which I took with me when I escaped from the island,' explained Amia.

'The prophecy states that the code of the Vortex could only be broken by the souls of purity. My name Amia stands for 'Good', and Avinash's name stands for 'Earth', so we knew the code, but before we had a chance to protect Zeneka, Zhakhan had already invaded the island with his curse of the swamp and then he captured Avinash, which is why, I then had to escape from the island.'

'But before I left, I protected Shrina and Kavi with the powers of purity from the Fountain of Innocence, so that if they had to face the Vortex alone, then they would not forget their memories, and they could also try to free the forgotten children and then try to solve the code.'

'So did you escape to Crystal Water Lake and that is how you met the Professor?' asked Isaac.

'Yes, Isaac,' replied Amia. 'A year ago, before the waters became a swamp, I chanted a prayer to the waters of Zeneka to allow the water to divide into two, so that our two worlds could collide when it became the final day of the century, so then I would have been able to return to the island with the sacred items to help Shrina and Kavi.'

'So how did you meet the Professor?' asked Tristan.

'The Professor found me. I was sitting alone playing my lute on the shores of the lake and he invited me to stay in his manor.'

'Did you tell him about Zeneka Island and about the prophecy?' asked Mariella.

'Yes, and because he wanted to help me, he chose to write a book about the island. Then he decided to hold a competition, but none of us ever thought that his adventure story would come true, because he did actually hide a statue of a green monkey in the grounds of the manor for you all to find.'

'The Professor was very clever though, because after I had told him about the prophecy, he was the one who worked out that if you all found the Green Monkey in the manor, before the final chime of the fifth hour, then our two worlds would not have needed to collide and then Lord Zhakhan would not have been able to enter the Vortex to win,' explained Amia.

'Even if he did manage to destroy time, he would only be able to rule Zeneka Island, but his greed would have no power to rule the rest of the world.'

'Oh, I see!' said Eva. 'The Vortex can only rise when good versus evil, so if his intention was just to bring evil to the Vortex without bearing any of his own gifts, then the Vortex would not have allowed him to enter. So, if you did return to Zeneka, and he tried to challenge you, Shrina and Kavi, without having a good reason to enter the Vortex, then the watch, the flute and the kaleidoscope would have protected all of you. You could have all then followed the colours of the circles to find the code of the Vortex.'

'Then when you had found all of the letters, you could have entered the word Mritsa at the final chime of the fifth hour, and your gift to the Vortex would have been the glass decanter because it was the sign of purity. Is that correct?'

'Yes, Eva, and although Zhakhan is a very clever man, he has become very greedy and he has ignored the rules of the prophecy and of the Vortex. So when he took your watch, the glass decanter and the coloured circles, and offered them as gifts to the Vortex, they were not his to give.'

'The Vortex is very powerful and very clever, which is why it zapped away the items, so that Lord Zhakhan could not use them against their rightful owners. But, if Zhakhan did still manage to get into the Vortex somehow, and then destroy time, then the Vortex would have been destroyed, but he would not have won his own desired quest to rule the rest of the world,' explained Amia.

'The purity of your souls is the only reason why the Vortex allowed you to keep the flute and the kaleidoscope,' added Avinash.

All of the children and the staff of the palace, formed into an orderly line and then, one-by-one, each person took it in turn to say their own private prayer to the God of Peace and then placed their candle on to the floor beneath the Fountain of Innocence, before returning to the palace to continue their celebration.

'So, if we had not been distracted by the lights that were in the lake, then we would still be searching for clues in the manor, which the Professor would have made up so that we could try to find the Green Monkey, but I'm so glad that we did get distracted, because we have been blessed to meet so many people from all over the world and we have still solved our quest, but the best bit is, that we actually found the real God of Peace - by having a real life adventure!' said Tristan, feeling very pleased.

'Yeah, Tristan, but after having *this* adventure, if our quest was only to just go looking around the manor for clues, well, don't you think that kind of makes the adventure seem quite dull and boring now?' laughed Isaac. 'And because we've been so lucky to have a real life adventure - the things in life that we will all come across as time goes by… will never ever be the same again!'

The four children and Shrina and Kavi joined in with all of the other children and danced around the palace ballroom in their glamorous clothes for what seemed like hours and hours of fun. As they danced, they all thought about their adventure and how amazing and clever the Professor's story really was.

'Do you know what? Not only did the Professor fulfil Queen Amia's dream, he also let us act out a part of our own stories that we gave him,' said Mariella. 'I have always dreamed of getting dressed up and dancing around and playing music.'

'Yes, you're right, Mariella,' replied Tristan, smiling. 'My story was about using my knowledge instead of having magical powers, and we all tricked Lord Zhakhan into thinking that we did have special powers, so it was his greed of taking our things that led us all to victory!'

'Yeah, and in my story, I said that I loved fast rides and adventure,' added Isaac. 'That rollercoaster ride that we had when we all got sucked into the lake, has got to be, by far, the greatest ride of my life! And if you think about it, my story also stated that I had to go through a maze of mirrors to get home. The Vortex was like a maze, and we all worked out how to break the code, and we helped Shrina and Kavi to free all of the other children too.'

'Yes, but the best bit of all was that Queen Amia got to go home to her family and that Zeneka Island has been saved. Professor Dowley is a truly kind-hearted man and he is such a generous and wonderful person. My story only told a tale of a real life dream that I had, which was all about having a happy ending - his marvellous adventure has given everyone a happy ending!' said Eva.

'Professor Dowley sounds like such a wonderful man, I hope that one day we will get to meet him too,' said Shrina with a smile.

'And I'm so glad that mother got to meet him, because he helped her to keep strong and his wonderful adventure story is also what has brought all of us together,' added Kavi.

'Will your family return to India, now that the island is safe?' asked Tristan.

'Yes, we can all go back to India now,' replied Shrina.

'So what will happen to Zeneka Island now?' asked Isaac.

'Zeneka, our beautiful island, will continue to move to different locations beneath the waters of the world and it will continue to remain hidden. Lord Hanuman will protect the palace and the island, just in case, anyone else tries to invade it again!' replied Kavi.

As the evening drew to an end, the music stopped playing and King Avinash made his final announcement to everyone.

'Thank you again, my people. Thank you to all of my Children of Time for saving Zeneka Island and for saving the time of our world. I must now ask you all to follow me to the sandy shores, so that I can let you all return back to your world. I promise you, that once you have all safely returned to your lands - the year of time that has once been lost, has now been restored. You will see when you return - that the time that it was just before your capture, will remain as exactly as the same time - and no amount of time will have been lost.'

Everyone followed the king and queen to the sandy shores at the front of the palace. As they all looked around for the final time at the beautiful sunset towering over the pure crystal blue water, Queen Amia quietly chanted over the waters. The water started to divide into two and what looked like a familiar watery staircase, suddenly once again appeared.

'Goodbye, my fair children. When you enter into the water, please do not be afraid, when you reach the bottom step, it will safely lead you back to your world and you will return to the surface of the water of where you were once playing,' said Queen Amia reassuring all of the children.

Tristan, Isaac, Mariella and Eva stopped to watch, as one-by-one all of the other children began to disappear into the water to go back to their worlds and, as they watched the last child leave, they became the only ones left on the island with the King, the Queen, Princess Shrina, Prince Kavi and all of the staff of the palace.

'Will we ever see you again?' whispered the children sadly.

'You have brought our worlds back together and I am pretty sure that time will never let you forget us, and whenever you hear music playing or any clocks chiming, it will remind you of us and of this glorious day,' replied King Avinash.

'Yes, and when you are all a bit older, maybe you can come and visit us in India,' said Queen Amia, smiling.

'Yes, that would be lovely, we would all definitely want to come to India to see you all again. Maybe we could all write to each other for now, so that we can keep in touch?' said Tristan happily.

'Oh yes, we must! That would be so exciting,' added Mariella. 'And it would be so lovely to see you all return to your royal kingdom and we would all love to see the beauty of India. Here is your flute, Queen Amia, I really loved playing your song and I will never ever forget it.'

Isaac then stepped forward and took out the kaleidoscope from his pocket and handed it back to Queen Amia.

'This kaleidoscope helped us to see what we really needed to see, at the right time and in the right place, and I am very honoured to have been chosen to use one of your sacred gifts. Thank you, Queen Amia,' said Isaac politely, as he handed back the gift.

Eva then took out the glass decanter and passed it over to Queen Amia.

'Queen Amia, do you mind if I ask you if it was your soul that was in the lake? Were you the Lady of the Lake?' asked Eva.

'No, I don't mind you asking me that, Eva,' said Amia.

'When I escaped, yes, I did leave a part of my soul above the surface of Crystal Water Lake so that when the time came for me to return here, my soul would have remained pure. I guess you could say that I may have been *a* lady of the lake, but there are many lost souls out there, Eva, which is why so many people often visit the lake - to feel peace.' replied Queen Amia.

'I want you to take this decanter back with you and please give it to Professor Dowley as a gift for his kindness and generosity, and so that he can keep it in his Hall of Treasures.'

'I can't give back the pocket watch because Lord Zhakhan has taken it with him,' said Tristan, feeling quite worried.

'Don't worry, Tristan,' replied King Avinash reassuringly. 'The watch is very powerful and he cannot destroy it, and I am sure that it will give my cousin plenty of time to see the error of his ways!'

'Is there *any way* that he can come back?' asked Isaac curiously.

'Well, it is very hard to answer that question, Isaac, lets hope not, but there are many stories in life, where people have often said that even when put in the most difficult of circumstances, a person's willpower can save them - *even* in their darkest hour!' replied King Avinash.

The children stood for a little while to watch the beautiful sunset over the calm blue waters and sighed with happiness as they took in the view of such peace and harmony. As they stood and watched, each child thought back to the adventure that they had just conquered and started to smile as their minds wandered back in time.

'That was a wonderful adventure, wasn't it?' said Mariella.

'Yes, it sure was, Mariella, especially the part where we won!' replied Isaac victoriously.

'Yes!' sighed Eva. 'Everyone was saved and everyone has had a happy ending!'

'Well, not quite everyone, Eva,' laughed Tristan. 'But yes, it was so nice to be able to help all of those children and, look, we also helped to restore the island, and *'Miss Deena'* was safe to return... to be the queen that she has always been to us!'

'I know I really shouldn't be saying this, but I can't help but feel sorry for Lord Zhakhan. I know he was in the wrong, but I bet, that somewhere deep down inside of him, there must be some good in his heart. I just hope that wherever he is now, that time will show him the error of his ways and then maybe he will turn into a better man,' said Mariella.

The four children hugged each of their new found friends, then walked towards the glowing open waters and then turned back to smile and wave together.

'Goodbye, everyone, we will all miss you and we hope to see you all again very soon,' shouted the children together before disappearing into the water and towards the light.

They walked downwards to the very bottom of the water steps, and as they reached the last step, they could all feel their ballroom clothes magically transforming back into their original adventure clothing!

They jumped one-by-one into a small gap, which then led them safely back into the water of Crystal Water Lake.

Taking a brief swim upwards, the children looked around underwater and found themselves swimming alongside some beautiful and very colourful fish.

The sight was truly astonishing as they floated upwards, whilst passing the views of some very beautiful wide flat fish, rainbow trout, pretty little sea horses and a few jelly fish, that bubbled all around them.

~ Chapter X ~

The Emerald Island

They safely swam to the top of the surface of Crystal Water Lake and found themselves back in familiar surroundings, now seeing the scenes of forestry and the large Rocky Mountains that surrounded the lake.

'Wow! What an adventure that was!' said Tristan.

'And look,' said Isaac. 'It's stopped raining now and the skies are all clear!'

'And look, the water has closed back up and there are no signs of any steps any more and the lights have disappeared too,' added Eva.

'But oh, doesn't it all look so peaceful and beautiful around here? A valuable lesson has been learned from this adventure, and I really think that from now on, we really should appreciate the wonders of life a little bit more in future,' said Mariella.

They all had a quick swim and splashed around in the water, laughing and playing together, and then they looked up at the distant clock of the manor.

However, for some reason, the time on the clock was now showing as 4.45pm!

'That's strange,' said Tristan, looking up at the clock. 'We solved our quest just before 5 o'clock, didn't we? And then we stayed later than that to party with the others. I wonder if the manor's clock is running slow.'

As they got out of the water, they saw that the rain that had previously fallen had now almost washed away their names that they had written in the sand.

The only letters that now remained were just;

T...I...M... and E...

'Wow, how awesome is that! Our full names have been washed away, but the first letters of our names are still here and oddly enough they spell out the word TIME!' shouted Isaac.

'That's definitely a bit strange, but don't you think it seems quite magical at the same time?' squealed Mariella.

'And look, there are our shoes on the shore! I almost forgot that we were even wearing any shoes, because we left them at the Vortex. I wonder how they got here?' said Eva, puzzled, whilst passing everyone their shoes.

'Well, I guess that's what you really do call magic,' replied Tristan, laughing. 'Well, Children of Time, I do believe that our quest is now over and that we really should be heading back to the manor now.'

As he spoke, he stretched out his hands to the others.

But it seemed as though the magic was not quite over yet!

As the children all held hands and started to make their way back up the steep gravelly hill, they turned back to take one last look at Crystal Water Lake and then saw that sunlight had suddenly appeared from nowhere, and was now starting to slowly set in the distance, and just by chance... they also caught a glimpse of a beautiful golden eagle in the sky - flying away gracefully!

Smiling at the beautiful sunset, they continued to walk through the forests, when suddenly each child could feel that their wet clothes were now instantly and quite mysteriously becoming dry!

Approaching Mritsa Manor, the children could see pretty little tea lights hanging in the beautiful gardens of marvel, and there were red petals spread out all across the gardens.

'Wow! This looks just like what we saw in Zeneka!' shouted out Tristan.

The children walked through the garden towards the front of the manor and they could hear music playing from inside. Entering the manor, the children took off their coats and their shoes and then made their way into The Hall of Treasures.

'Come in, children, come, come!' came Professor Dowley's voice from his chair.

As the music finished playing, the clocks began to chime, announcing the fifth hour before then going very quiet and silencing all of the rooms of the manor.

'Professor, how is it that the clocks are all chiming now? I'm pretty sure it was five o'clock when we were in Zeneka Island, so surely the final chime of the fifth hour has already *been* played?' asked Tristan, very puzzled.

'Well, if memory serves *me* well, young Master Tristan, I do believe that you did ask time to wait for you - until you had finished your quest! The time when you conquered your quest in Zeneka Island was indeed 5pm, but if you remember back to when you first got here, the clocks chimed at 4.45pm, so when you asked time to wait for you - that was the time here. It appears that time has honoured your request until you have reached back here to Mritsa!' answered the Professor, standing up.

Although that seemed a little bit odd, it actually did seem to make sense to all of the children and they all looked at each other and nodded in agreement.

'First, let me congratulate you all for completing a fantastic adventure and for valiantly capturing every chapter of my book with such excellence!' he said, as he handed them each a certificate and then a copy of his *completed* book, 'The Emerald Island.'

'But… how did you know that all of this was really going to happen?' asked Isaac in total amazement.

'Well… a good magician never tells his secrets, my boy,' chuckled the Professor, winking at Isaac.

'Professor, will we see Miss Deena, I mean Queen Amia, King Avinash, Princess Shrina and Prince Kavi ever again?' asked Mariella sadly.

'Well, in life, Miss Mariella, we are given many opportunities to meet many wonderful people, so I have always believed that paths can always cross again - *however* mysterious the circumstances may seem!' replied the Professor.

'Professor, Queen Amia told me to give you the decanter as a gift for your Hall of Treasures,' said Eva, passing over the glass bottle. 'What would have happened if we didn't find the island, and if we didn't find the Green Monkey here in the manor before the final chime of the fifth hour?' quizzed Eva.

'That is a very good question, Miss Eva. Well, let me see,' he said, pacing around the room as he spoke.

'My adventures of life happened when I was a young boy, so when I started writing novels, I realised that adventures could only happen if you really wanted them to. So I can really only say that life experiences through the eyes of a child - can create the most marvellous ideas when fantasy combines with reality!'

'Now in answer to your question, Miss Eva, if you didn't find the island, it would not have mattered, as your clues have been in the manor all along, which I am pretty sure - you have all worked that out by now?' said the Professor, looking at all of the children.

'I had absolutely no doubts at all, because I believed that you would have all found a way to solve your quest! As I said from the very beginning, with knowledge comes great power, and that your memory would serve you well. It appears that you have all unknowingly paid attention to my riddles - but in the end, Miss Eva, it really was only down to you all to experience an adventure of a lifetime. I believe that it was your desire and courage which led you all to win.'

'It was the purity of your innocence that led you all to a greater destiny. How do you think you would have solved the riddles if you didn't find the Emerald Island?' asked the Professor, whilst curiously looking at all four of them.

'Well,' said Isaac. 'Before we became distracted by the lights near the lake - when we were outside in the garden, I was thinking that we should follow the colour code of a rainbow, and then I imagined that we would have run into a few of your staff, who would possibly have been dressed up as a character from your book.'

'Then, I think we would have had to exchange one of our coloured circles with them for a clue, which would obviously be in a riddle and when we had worked out that riddle, it would have then led us towards the next clue, where we would have then had to swap the next coloured circle. Is that right Professor?'

'Yes, my masterful Curious One. As you can see, that it would have been the curiosity of your knowledge and your desire to find out if your idea was correct, that would have put you all on the right path to start your adventure,' replied the Professor, smiling. 'And where exactly do you think you would have looked first, Isaac?'

'Well, I think the first circle was going to be in the forest, because it was the only place which was *not* as colourful as the rest of your gardens, and it may have been J.J. who would have been the one to swap my red circle for a clue. Would I have been right?' replied Isaac.

'Excellent thinking, my boy!' shouted the Professor. 'Yes, that would have been all correct, Master Isaac, but I would now like to make a suggestion to you all. Always remember that':

"An apple never falls far from a tree!"

'I think that the first clue that J.J would have given us would be the saying 'with knowledge comes great power', which would have been a little bit confusing because we already had a note from you saying the same thing, but it would have made us think twice about where to go next, and I think that would have led us to the library, which of course is the place of great knowledge!' said Eva.

'And I think that we would have had to search through all of your many books to find another clue, which would then have required us to swap the yellow circle - the circle of wisdom! Is that right Professor?'

'Miss Eva, the Visionary One! Yes, that is absolutely correct,' replied the Professor. 'So my next advice to you all is to remember to':

"Never judge a book by its cover!"

'And I think that our next clue would have had information about happiness and the clue may have said something that would have led us to your pink room in The Hall of Treasures, because the clue would have said something inside of it to remind us that life can sometimes be like a show! Is that correct Professor?' asked Mariella.

'Yes, Mariella, happiness can bring all sorts of excitement to life's little dramas,' laughed the Professor. 'So children, no matter where you find yourselves in life, always remember that':

"The show must go on!"

'That means, our next clue would have led us outside to the water garden!' said Tristan, very excitedly. 'We would have had the green circle next, so what better place could there be to swap a green circle other than by the fish pond? The place where you have all of God's real life creatures both great and small, living together in peace and harmony. Is that correct?'

'Very well deciphered, Master Tristan!' replied the Professor.

'Now children, the next saying that I have for all of you, is an ultimate message - a message that will give you the most precious meanings of life!'

'You must *always* remember that':

"In order to find peace and happiness-
One must first live one's life!"

'Yes, that's so true Professor!' shouted out Isaac, dying to say the details of the next clue. 'So we would have swapped the orange circle in the front entrance of the manor, where it looks like a chess board! That is the only room of the manor which had the look of an adventure in it. Is that right?'

'Oh, Curious One that loves adventures the most!' laughed the Professor. 'Yes, Master Isaac, quite valiantly spotted! A game of chess does require its players to be very skilful, cunning and wise. So, it would be also very wise for you all to remember that whether you win or lose, it really doesn't matter because':

"It's never about the game - It's how you
play it that counts!"

'Oh, this is really exciting!' squealed Mariella.

'So I think the clues for the next two circles, would've been found in different places - 2 very different places, which we really wouldn't have thought about so quickly, because those circles seemed to be quite similar. Your last 2 rooms in the Hall of Treasures, Professor, did not seem to have a theme going on in them, like the other rooms did - so we assumed that those two rooms were a combination of happy and sad times in your life.'

'So, I think we would've had to swap the purple circle in a swamp, because that would have been a dark place, and the blue circle, would've had to have been swapped in this actual hall, because it's your happy place. Is that right, Professor?'

'Excellent answer Miss Mariella, Yes, that is very, very true and very, very correct! I have lived a very happy and prosperous life and I have taken so many journeys, but I do always try to remind *myself* that':

"All that glitters is not gold!"

'Your riddles are excellent, Professor!' said Tristan. 'When we first got here, we could not understand the meanings of any of the riddles in the scroll, but now everything makes so much more sense. You're a genius and your quest has been absolutely brilliant!'

'Yes, yes you are, Professor! You're absolutely brilliant!' said the others, all joining in to agree with Tristan.

'Thank you very, very much, my wise and clever adventurers,' replied the Professor, feeling quite overwhelmed by their kindness.

'So when we would have found the first seven clues, a clue from your Hall would have then led us to the music room where we would have had to find a musical manuscript, so that I could play its song, and then by working out the name of the song, we would have been led nearer to our last clues! Is that right, Professor?' asked Mariella.

'Yes, my sweet Melodic One, that is correct. As I said before, no-one knows what lies behind the power of music! So it would have been your musical talent and your knowledge, that would have helped you all to work out that the power of music can quite often spell out a thousand words!' replied the Professor.

'Aah! So by finding the right song, we would have then been led to somewhere where we could find a message that would say - 'only purity of the soul may walk in victory!' said Eva. 'And I think we would've kind of found a combination of 2 clues there, where one of the clues would've had something to do with *time* and the other, would've led us towards something that was *pure.*'

'Excellent thinking, Miss Eva!' replied the Professor.

'So the first clue, would've led us to search every single clock in the manor until we had found all of the letters that we would have needed to spell out the words - 'destiny lies upon good earth'. Is that right?' asked Tristan.

'Correct, my boy! Now do you see why 'Time takes only Time'?' asked the Professor.

'Yes, now I do Professor. Time waits for no-one!' said Tristan. 'It was our adventure all along, and we all knew that we could not *really* stop time, but if we required more time, then all we had to do was ask! When we first came to the manor and when we heard the clocks chime early in the Hall of Treasures, it was just a sign to let us know that we could've had more time if we needed it.'

'We all remembered that time was of the essence and as we would have followed the clues one-by-one, we would have learned a valuable lesson of life - which was, to just remember that by using our knowledge, we would've ended up in the right place at the right time.'

'So every clock that possessed a correct letter, would have chimed, because we were in the right place at the right time. Is that correct, Professor?'

'Exactly, my valiant Keeper of Time! No-one can ever tell how any adventure can come about, nor can they identify how *real* it could turn out to be. So, now you have all learned that fortune favours only the brave! You became lost between two worlds, but in life, it takes great strength and great courage to ask for help, but you were not afraid to ask for help when the time was right for you,' said the Professor.

'Yes and the second clue would've prompted us to search for purity! At the very start of our adventure, when we were first looking around, I counted that there were six water fountains in the back garden and there was the one in the front of the manor, so in total, there were - *seven pure water fountains!* The glass decanter has always been full of *pure water*, so we would've had to search all six of the water fountains first to get our final clue.'

'I think we would have found a clear circle in each of the six fountains, which Isaac would then have had to put into his kaleidoscope to see what letter was inscribed on each of them. So when we would have tried to decipher all of the six letters, they hopefully, would have spelled out the word Mritsa.'

'Then *that* would have led us to your main water fountain at the front of the garden, where we would've found the Green Monkey - in the manor's 'Fountain of Innocence!' continued Eva.

'And because we were in the right place, at the right time, we would've learned, that the Green Monkey was amongst the colourful garden, which is *your* 'Rainbow Full of Dreams,' Professor - a place where all colours unite as one! Is that correct, Professor?'

'Absolutely Correct! My sweet Visionary One! I couldn't have put it any better myself!'

'But if at some point we were going in the wrong direction, then we would've come across the characters of Shrina and Kavi, who would have helped us.'

'So I'm guessing that Goola Bala Swamp is just a place somewhere around here, that you have invented, so that, if the person who was playing the character of Lord Zhakhan did manage to catch us, then we would have ended up in the swamp and we would have lost the game. Is that right, Professor?' asked Isaac.

'Yes, yes, yes!' laughed the Professor. 'So now you can all see, that my riddles are really *not* quite as difficult as they may seem!'

'Professor, would you mind if we quickly run around your manor to find the clues for the game that we should have played here in Mritsa Manor, as I think it would be so amazing for us to collect the answers that we would have found, just so that we can see for ourselves how clever we were to find all of the clues?' asked Isaac.

'I had my suspicions that you would say that,' laughed the Professor. 'Of course you may, my young adventurers. Yes, that is a very good idea, because I have always taught myself to remember that':

"Stories can only unfold…when someone fulfils an adventure!"

Smiling, he looked at them, knowing that each one was thinking exactly the same thing as Isaac.

'The time is now exactly 5.15 pm, so I'll see you all in the front garden - let's say, in about forty five minutes. Okay? Oh and Isaac, I think that you might be needing these,' said the Professor, pulling out *another* seven coloured circles from his pocket, and then he handed them over to Isaac.

The children passed their books back to the Professor for safe keeping and then Tristan pulled out the scroll from his pocket and handed it back to the Professor, and then they all ran off as fast as they could towards the forest!

Thinking what the Professor had just said to them, Isaac led the others to a group of trees. 'The Professor just said, that an apple never falls far from a tree! Quick, search all of the apple trees,' he shouted.

Sure enough, as they started hunting through the trees, Isaac called out, 'Here it is! There's a note here, and it's the first clue!'

'Quick, read it out, Isaac,' said an excited Tristan.

'It's in italic writing,' said Isaac. 'It says';

'With Great Knowledge, Comes Great Power!'

'That says exactly the same thing as the note that we already have - with great knowledge comes great power,' laughed Tristan, pulling out the other note from his pocket.

'Quick, everyone, let's head for the library!' said Eva.

Isaac left his red circle by the tree and then they all ran as fast as they could back into the manor and straight into the huge library.

'Wow! Just look at all of the books that he has in here! Which one do you think the next clue is in?' asked Tristan.

'That's easy!' laughed Eva. 'Remember, the Professor said right from the start that memory would serve us well didn't he? Well, what he meant by that, was that we had to remember everything that we had heard by everyone and not just by him!'

'Yeah, you're right, Eva, but no-one said anything about the library, did they?' quizzed Isaac.

'No! But J.J. did mention a book, in fact, he mentioned a specific book - 'The Gardens of Marvel.' Does that ring any bells?' laughed Eva.

'Oh Yeah, you're so clever, Eva! Quick, let's hunt for the Gardens of Marvel!' shouted Isaac.

The children split up and searched the very big room and scanned every bookshelf to look at the names of every single book until they found what they were looking for, when suddenly a voice called out.

'Here it is!' yelled Mariella, opening up the book and taking out the next piece of paper.

'By Drawing Curtains - One Can Often Reveal Many Different Scenes!'

'The next clue says; by drawing curtains, one can often reveal many different scenes. You know what that means don't you?' laughed Mariella.

'The next clue is in my favourite room - the pink room in The Hall of Treasures, because that's a type of theatre room.'

Isaac then left the yellow circle on a coffee table in the Library, and they headed for The Hall of Treasures.

'Look, the hall's been decorated up, I wonder if there's going to be a party in here later?' said Mariella.

They walked slowly into the pink room and then carefully searched it, as they did not want to break anything.

As they hunted around looking at all of the puppets and dolls, Tristan noticed a beautiful model of a theatre house on the table. He saw a wind-up key on the back of it and turned it.

A sweet tune started to play and, as it did, it made the closed curtains on it open up, which revealed a little stage, and there on it was the next clue!

'To Survive Under Water - One Must First Learn How To Swim!'

'Guys, here's the next clue! It says; to survive under water, one must first learn how to swim. The Water Garden is where we're heading next,' Tristan said, smiling.

The children were even more excited now and they were absolutely loving this adventure, but what they loved the most, was being allowed to run in and out of the manor so many times.

The children then began to realise that by having to go in and out of the manor so many times - was the Prosessor's clever way of creating a maze... just like a Vortex!

Isaac left the pink circle in the pink room and then they raced outside and went to the largest pond at the back of the water garden.

'This is where life breathes,' said Eva. 'This is where all of God's creatures, both great and small, can live happily together in peace and harmony.'

'Here's the next clue! It's behind these garden gnomes,' shouted Isaac.

'To Play Any Game - One Must First Understand The Rules!'

'It says; to play any game, one must first understand the rules!' said Isaac. 'Well, it looks like we're all off to your favourite room next then, Tristan - the chess-styled room in the entrance of the manor!' laughed Isaac, leaving the green circle by one of the gnomes.

They ran back quickly to the front of the manor to search the exquisite large room, which was very tidy and uncluttered. As they looked around, Eva found a clear vase full of fresh flowers, but behind it, was the next clue which had been cleverly engraved on a plaque behind the vase.

'To Seek Light - One Must First Battle Through Darkness!'

'Here it is,' said Eva. 'It says; to seek light, one must first battle through darkness.'

'Aah! Now this where we have to find two riddles, because we only have the purple and blue circles left,' said Mariella.

'Yes, you're right, Mariella. These next two clues are about the Professor's journeys,' replied Tristan.

'I guess the purple circle will be somewhere dark and lonely - like a swamp perhaps?' said Eva.

'Yes and the blue one is going to be in a happy place - like The Hall of Treasures!' added Mariella.

Isaac left the orange circle by the flower vase and then they raced down the gardens again, this time searching all of the many gardens of the manor until they reached the very bottom of the front gardens, where they found an area which was full of mud!

'Well, we certainly have found the lonely, dark place!' laughed Isaac. 'Look over there, on that fence, there is a lantern hanging above it. That must be the light! There's no point in all of us getting dirty, I'll go through the mud and get it. Okay?'

He waded through the gooey, damp and very cold wet mud until he reached the lantern. He opened a little door at the back of it and, sure enough, inside of it was another clue!

Isaac picked up the note and left the purple circle on top of the fence and then made his way back to the others.

'Destiny Holds a Rainbow Full of Dreams!'

'It says; destiny holds a rainbow full of dreams - and I think that we all know by now, that the rainbow is in the Hall of Treasures! Oh he's so clever, isn't he?' said Eva, reading out the note.

They knew that they only had limited time to find all of the clues, but through having so much fun, they suddenly looked over at the manor's clock and saw that half an hour had passed already!

'Come on, guys, we only have about fifteen minutes left - we've nearly finished our quest, but we really do have to be quick now,' said Tristan.

They ran really fast back to the manor and straight back in to the Hall of Treasures. When they arrived there to look around, in the top drawer of the Professor's writing desk, they found another clue.

'A Voice From Within - Can Make Any Heart Sing!'

'It says; a voice from within, can make any heart sing. Quick, we need to head for the music room,' said Isaac, whilst leaving his final circle on the Professor's writing desk.

Parting with the last of the seven circles, they raced off towards the music room, and they felt very excited now, because they knew that they were so close to conquering their quest!

As they entered in to the music room, they all searched very quickly to try to find a song sheet for Mariella to play. As Mariella looked around, she saw an elegant picture on the wall which was full of hearts, stars and musical notes, and as she stared at it more closely, she could then see that it also contained a hidden but very cleverly disguised song manuscript within it!

'I've found it, I've found the manuscript! Look at this picture everyone. The manuscript has been very cleverly hidden in this picture!' she shouted.

'Whoa, that's really cool!' said Isaac. 'Now all we need to do is find you an instrument to play.'

'Aah! Of course,' said Eva smiling, from the other side of the room. 'I think I have just found the voice from within!' she shouted out.

She then pointed to a red, heart shaped box which was sat upon a silvery coloured, star-shaped plaque.

Mariella walked over to the red box which was patterned in golden coloured musical notes and as she opened it, inside of it was a silver flute!

'Oh, look how sweet this box is, and look there's a flute in here!' said Mariella.

She then picked up the flute and began to play the notes that she could see on the manuscript. It sounded like such a beautiful song and as she played it, she suddenly started to recognise it.

The song was called 'Twin Angels' and it was one of her favourites, because it was a song that she and her twin sister would sing together all the time, *and* it was the same tune that she had played earlier in the Chambers of Time in Zeneka Island!

As she finished playing, she felt rather overwhelmed that the Professor had somehow let a part of her sister be in the adventure with her.

'He's so wonderful! I really don't know how he does it,' she cried. 'The name of the song is called Twin Angels, and our next clue is going to be on the gates of the manor! There are twin angels on either side of the black gates. I noticed them when we first drove in.'

They raced off to the gates of the manor, and there either side of the gates, were twin angels just as Mariella had said that she had seen.

They all looked up at the closed gates. In the arch-shaped section of the gates there was an inscription written there:

'Only Purity Of The Soul May Walk In Victory'

'This is what he meant when he said that beauty can surpass all evil. Angels are always placed on the gates of heaven to keep bad at bay, and only a pure soul can enter into heaven!' replied Mariella.

'Oh, well how clever is that!' said Tristan. 'And look here, there's a sun dial and it has an inscription on it, *and* the dial is pointing upwards, towards the manor's clock!

'Only In The Hands Of Time - Can One Truly Fulfil One's Desires'

'It says; only in the hands of time, can one truly fulfil one's desires! Quick guys, we only just about have enough time to search for our desires! Right, we need to find every single letter for our next clue, but because there are so many clocks in there, let's split up and when we've found all of the letters, let's meet back in the entrance. Okay?'

Their journey was almost coming to an end, so they raced back into the manor. The boys ran to search all of the clocks upstairs, and the girls stayed downstairs. As the search went on, there were a lot of loud chiming sounds coming from the correct clocks that contained a letter, and it really did sound very musical!

The boys found twelve letters upstairs and the girls found twelve letters downstairs. They quickly all met back up in the hallway and spread out the pieces of paper containing the letters, onto the black and white chess board floor and sure enough, when all of the letters were placed in to the correct order, they spelt out the words:

'Destiny Lies Upon Good Earth'

Now everyone was getting really excited because they knew exactly where to go to find the final clue!

They raced to the six fountains in the back garden and then quickly collected the six clear circles that they each managed to find inside all of the fountains.

'But I don't have the kaleidoscope any more,' said Isaac.

'It doesn't matter, Isaac,' said Eva. 'Remember, it's how we *play* the game that counts, and we have all played the game very well - we have found all of the clues *and* all of the answers! The coloured circles and these clear circles, really only have the same meaning as my glass decanter. What I mean by that is, as we were playing the game, somewhere along the line, we all somehow started to understand the rules, which is why everything then started to become more *clearer* to us - so that is how it became easier for us to find all of the answers!'

'Oh yeah!' shouted the others.

Finally, as they all realised that everything was now *clear* to them, they then quickly all raced back to the front garden of the manor.

There waiting for them, was Professor Dowley, and behind him, were his staff members - who were all dressed up as fancy dress characters!

The children felt so excited, as they knew that they had now finished their quest, but just to add to all of the excitement, the Professor was about to hold a party for *them* and it was going to be a fancy dress party!

Walking over to the Professor, the children handed over the six clear circles to him, and then they all started to speak together.

'Everything is now, *very clear to us*, Professor!

The children then found themselves chanting out their answer in rhyme:

'*M* is for Memories
R is for Rhyme
I am the only one
T hat can battle with time
S ongs of life, reveal prayers of gold
A dventures are all stories… which in time shall unfold'

'The code which completes our quest, Professor - is **Mritsa!**' said all of the children together, as they smiled and then gave out a big sigh of relief.

Just as they spoke, the clocks all began to chime on the sixth hour!

'Well done, children, well done! You are all the winners of your quest and all of your answers are completely correct! Marvellous!' beamed the Professor.

'So, congratulations for the second time,' he laughed. 'Now you can see, that you have all managed to play the same game twice - but in two *very* different worlds! You will also be able to see in the copy of your books - that I have written *your* adventure story in exactly the same way that you have just played the game!'

The children looked at the Professor in astonishment, as they could not believe that he knew what they were thinking! And more to the point - how on earth did he know... how *they* even thought that they should've played the game?

They then each looked inside of the cover of their own book, and saw that a personal message had been written for all of them inside of the book.

The message had also been personally signed by the Professor.

For My Dearest Children of Time,

Congratulations for solving your quest!

Remember... with great knowledge, comes great power
Beauty shines only from within your soul
Behind every journey lies an untold story
Fortune favours only the brave
Always look forward to your destiny!

With regards,

Patrick Joseph Michael Dowley

Professor Patrick Joseph Michael Dowley

'Take a look and see if you are right,' said the Professor smiling, as he stood by the main water fountain.

The children then looked very closely at the fountain. They could now see the word *MRITSA* very cleverly engraved into the circular grey stone of the fountain.

As they all stared at the flowing fountain... there it was!

Sitting right in the centre of the fountain, was a very small green statue, in the shape of... The Green Monkey!

Isaac then curiously asked, 'Professor, so what will happen to Lord Zhakhan now?'

The Professor turned around to face the children, and then he smiled and winked at all of them.

'That, I believe...would be another story, don't you think?'